BURNED
Book Four in the Forbidden Series

By
Melody Anne

BURNED

Book Four in the Forbidden Series

ISBN-13: 978-1502771131
ISBN-10: 1502771136

Cover Art by Edward
Edited by Alison
Interior Design by Adam

www.melodyanne.com

Email: info@melodyanne.com

 /MelodyAnneAuthor  @AuthMelodyAnne

First Edition
Printed in the USA

DEDICATION

This is dedicated to my good friend, Ruth Cardello who inspires me to be a better writer, who makes me dance, and who can *shake it off* all the way down the streets of Edinburgh. I adore you!

NOTE FROM THE AUTHOR

We are inspired by so many different people and events in our lives. I could never write without the help of my family and friends from near and far. Thank you to those who have been with me from the beginning and those who are new in my life. I adore all of you and I rely on you. I hope you all enjoy the conclusion to the Forbidden series. Tyler has been a fun character to write, as he has a little bit of naughty and a lot of nice.

Melody Anne

OTHER BOOKS BY MELODY ANNE

Billionaire Bachelors:
*The Billionaire Wins the Game
*The Billionaire's Dance
*The Billionaire Falls - Amazon
*The Billionaire's Marriage Proposal
*Blackmailing the Billionaire
*Run Away Heiress
*The Billionaire's Final Stand
*Unexpected Treasure
*Hidden Treasure
*Holiday Treasure

Baby for the Billionaire:
*The Tycoon's Revenge
*The Tycoon's Vacation
*The Tycoon's Proposal
*The Tycoon's Secret
*The Lost Tycoon

Surrender:
*Surrender - Book One
*Submit - Book Two
*Seduced - Book Three
*Scorched - Book Four

Forbidden Series:
*Bound -Book One
*Broken - Book Two
*Betrayed - Book Three
*Burned - Book Four

Unexpected Heroes:
*Her Unexpected Hero
*Who I am With You - Novella
*Her Hometown Hero - Amazon (June 30th 2015)
*Following Her - Novella
*Her Forever Hero - Amazon (March 2016)

*Safe in His Arms - Novella - Baby, It's Cold Outside Anthology

PROLOGUE

"WE'LL BE BEST friends forever, right?"

A very young Tyler Knight, then age thirteen, turned to look at ten-year-old Elena Truman with a raised eyebrow and crooked grin that later in life would be one of his most recognizable expressions.

"I can't be best friends with a girl," he told her with a youthful attempt at a scoff.

"You promised we were best friends."

"Okay, we're best friends, but that's only between us. If my brothers knew I was best friends with a girl, they'd pummel me," Tyler said as he kicked the hard clump of dirt in front of him. "They'd mock me mercilessly."

"That's not fair, Tyler."

"Life's not fair. Get used to it."

"Why are you being so mean to me right now?" Tears filled Elena's young eyes.

"I'm older now. I'm a *teenager*, and my brothers said that girls are for one thing only."

"Huh? What thing is that?"

He looked away from her. "You know, the kissing and touching kind of thing," he said nervously.

"Why do girls and boys have to do that?" she replied. "It's stupid. Icky."

"It's just what they do, Lanie. See, that's why we can't be friends. You're too much of a baby."

1

"I can kiss!" she insisted. "I'm not a baby."

"Prove it," he said, and he stepped closer.

Her heart was racing a million miles a minute as her best friend, the boy she'd been inseparable from for five years, was now only a couple of inches away from her.

"Just do it," she said. Elena was so afraid of losing him.

He leaned forward and then he was pressing his closed lips against hers. Neither of them moved; they just stood there with their lips touching, their hands at their sides. They didn't have a clue what was supposed to come next.

He finally took a step back and Elena opened her eyes. That wasn't so bad after all. In fact, she could do that again.

"See, we can still be friends," she told him with a bright smile.

"That *was* stupid, Lanie. You don't know how to kiss," he said with a look she'd never seen on his face before.

The tears that had been threatening her earlier now spilled over. "You don't either, Tyler," she sniffled.

"Why don't you grow up before you come around again, little girl?"

"Fine. I don't want to be your friend anyway. You're a big jerk," she told him before turning and stumbling several steps away. "And you're the one who needs to grow up." She took off running, refusing to analyze whether she'd been shouting or wailing when she said those last few words.

"Good riddance," Tyler called after her, making her heart break even more.

Boys were nothing but trouble.

CHAPTER ONE

Ten Years Later

ELENA KNEW HER boss wasn't going to be happy with her, knew she was about to lose her job, but she had a point to prove. And the point was that she wasn't just a piece of meat. She had a respectable quantity of gray matter in her head. A lot more than that, if you wanted to get technical.

Yes, she needed the money, but after working at the gentleman's club for the past six month, she'd come to realize that the tips simply weren't worth the harassment. Yes, she'd make a lot less at any other waitressing job, but surely her pride was worth more than the few extra dollars that she could make by exposing her assets in a uniform that was far too tight and far too skimpy.

Men didn't normally look at her, and they certainly didn't lust after her — not unless she was dressed the way the club wanted her to be dressed. She was taller than the average woman; she stood at five foot eight, and even at age twenty, she hadn't yet grown into her body. Sadly, at least in her humble opinion, she appeared more gangly than womanly. The tomboy curse had apparently pursued her long past puberty.

Looking into the mirror, she pushed back her long dark hair before gathering it up into a severe knot on top of her head. She actually liked her hair, one of the few things she did like about herself.

She knew she was much too thin, but that was genetics. There wasn't anything she could do about it unless she wanted to mainline cinnamon rolls. Her hips were too narrow, her breasts too small. If it weren't for padded bras, the gentleman's club most likely wouldn't have hired her in the first place.

Her mother always told her that she was a flower, or rather a beautiful flower bud that someday would bloom. Elena was still waiting for that to happen. The only time it seemed that men gave her attention was when she was dolled up at the club. And that wasn't the kind of attention she wanted.

Why didn't she just quit this job? Well, she was going to. But not before making a point. Coming onto the floor looking less than sexy would infuriate her boss. Good. He deserved it.

She was finally ready. Looking in the mirror at an outfit that was too large, makeup that was practically nonexistent, and a hairstyle that was intentionally disastrous, she knew she'd be lucky to make it past the back room tonight without a confrontation.

After taking a deep breath, she stepped through the door, looking straight ahead, ignoring the shocked gasps from her co-workers. Hey, they were most likely pleased by her appearance. It certainly meant more tips for them.

But at least tonight her ass wouldn't be grabbed, and the "gentlemen" — yeah, right — wouldn't be soliciting her like she was their personal call girl. Some of the women who worked there would go home with the men. Maybe they'd even end up with jewelry, cars, housing, if they played it right. Elena wasn't that girl.

Though she knew she would never be a trophy wife, the kind of woman a captain of industry wanted on his arm, she also knew that she'd eventually marry a kind man — a regular guy — and have the life that she'd dreamed of having since childhood. A life completely unlike what she'd seen at home.

She hadn't had a bad life after her father had walked out on her mother and her. And her mom had never been bitter, had never told her not to find her own love. She'd just warned Elena that the world was full of frogs who couldn't be transformed by kisses, and that she should never settle for someone slimy. If they were all hands, it was because they wanted one thing. They were sticky, but with no sticking power.

When a group of men filled the club with their laughter as they walked in, Elena glanced in their direction. That's when her heart stopped beating for a moment. Before it sped up double time.

Tyler Knight.

If she hadn't decided to come to work tonight, had simply quit as she should have done, she wouldn't be going through the heartbreak of seeing her first love. In a gin joint like this. A titty bar, really, though hers had never been on display. Her heart thudded as she looked his way. She had only been ten when he'd broken her heart. And she'd tried not to think of him since.

It hadn't worked.

She'd followed him for years through the news and entertainment media. Like a kicked puppy, dammit. Why? Because he was her first love, her first best friend, the only person to this day she'd ever been fully open with — well, besides her mother and Piper, who had now taken Tyler's place in the best-friend stakes. She'd instantly bonded with Piper two years ago, their freshman year at the university.

"That's your table," one of the waitresses said before patting Elena on the shoulder. "Good luck."

"You take it," Elena replied.

"Are you sure? That's the youngest Knight brother, and that's the son of the junior senator. You know those tips are going to be big," said her co-worker, Sara, with hungry eyes. "Humongous."

"I'm positive," Elena told her. "I think I've made a mistake coming in tonight"

"Yeah, what's up with the appearance?" Sara asked.

"Trying to prove a point — that I'm not a piece of meat."

"Honey, to the men who come in here, that's exactly what we are," Sara said with a laugh. "And since they pay for my house and all the little baubles I'm so fond of, I really don't give a damn."

"That's the difference between us," Elena murmured. "Nothing is worth this to me."

"Good luck out in the real world, sweetie," Sara said before skipping over to the table and taking the men's orders, giggling and jiggling all the way.

"My office, now!" Her manager had spotted her, and he'd snarled those outraged words into her ear before he moved to the other side of the room.

Keeping her head down, she began slinking through the room, but she made a fatal mistake. She went by the group of guys she'd tried to avoid. And they were already drunk and rowdy.

"Why are you dressed down like this, darling?" One of the men at the table grabbed Elena's arm and held on. "I've seen you looking so much hotter before. How are we supposed to check out the merchandise when you're hiding your best stuff under mountains of material?"

Another one spoke up. "I want to see your nice set of tatas, babe."

The rest of the men cackled when the guy who'd grabbed her arm tugged and made her to fall into his lap. Elena was mortified as she struggled to break free. When her eyes connected with Tyler's for the first time in ten years, what she saw broke her heart all over again. And his words hit her even harder.

"This place has a much better selection of women to flirt with, Tom," Tyler said. "Why don't you let this one go so we can have a little fun?" Her former friend leaned back and smiled right at her.

When the group of men guffawed again, Elena's humiliation was complete. She never should have come back to this place, never should have put herself through this. Although she had a good poker face, self-confidence had never been one of her strong suits, and she'd just lost all her cards.

Yes, she'd been trying to prove that silly point — that she wasn't a piece of meat — but she also didn't need to be discarded like a lame horse. Tom released her, then slapped her ass as she struggled off his lap. Thank heaven for tender mercies, she told herself. At least he hadn't gone for her "tatas."

"I told you to come to my office!" Her manager was back with her. He was moving less than three feet from the men at the table, who were watching her further humiliation.

"I got mauled on my way there," she told him.

"Are you insulting our guests?" her manager asked far too loudly.

"I was the one who was insulted."

"You're position here is terminated. I want you out of my club immediately."

Laughter erupted again from the group of men who'd just humiliated her. This night couldn't possibly get any worse. Elena walked straight to the back room. The game she'd begun was over. She just wanted to leave.

Throwing a thick coat over her large uniform, she wiped away the tear that was streaking down her face and then grabbed her purse and slipped out the back door.

She didn't make it two feet before she heard a whistle. "Where are you off to in such a hurry, baby?"

A tremble ran through Elena when she heard that voice again. She was grateful to be in the shadows as she turned to face Tyler Knight for the second time that evening.

"I'm not your baby," she grated out.

"Wait! Don't go. I need to talk to you."

The alley was dark, making it impossible to read Tyler's expression. She knew she should turn and walk away — hell, stomp away was more like it — but for some reason, she found herself waiting.

"What do you want?"

"I was an asshole in there. I only did it so my friend would quit pawing at you like that. I could see it was making you uncomfortable."

"Why should you care?"

"Because we're at a gentleman's club. We should act as such."

Elena was too stumped to know how to deal with that remark.

"You're drunk," she told him. "I'd suggest that you go home." And she turned away.

"Wait!"

She stopped again. What was wrong with her? "I really want to get out of here," she said. "I just got manhandled by your friend, dissed, and then fired. I've had better days."

He was suddenly right in front of her. Elena took a step back, and her heart was hammering in her chest. He was far too close.

"Come have a drink with me. You can talk about it and I'll help make it better."

He lifted his hand and trailed his fingers down the side of her cheek, making a shiver race all through her body. She wasn't a little girl any longer, and this wasn't a childhood crush.

"There's no way I'm going back into that place," she said. Her voice and her body were trembling with disgust.

"I have my car right here. Come sit with me and have a drink."

His voice was mesmerizing, and without much thought she found her hand in his as he led her to the car. It wasn't until they climbed into the backseat — it wasn't a car, dammit; it was a limo! — and she found a glass with amber liquor in it in her hand that she realized what she was doing.

"What about your friends?"

"They're going to be busy for quite a while. They won't even notice that I'm gone."

"Is it a special occasion?"

"My buddy is getting married," he said with a laugh. "We'll celebrate next at his divorce."

"That's an odd thing to say." She drank the brandy and didn't think twice when he refilled her glass. She was too pleased with the way it helped numb her overwrought emotions after such a dreadful evening. A buzz wasn't such a bad thing.

"I don't believe in marriage, little lady. My parents' marriage was a disaster. No, the word *disaster* can't possibly capture the depths of that relationship and the way it turned out. And I don't see the point to a piece of paper. We all make our own paths. I choose to be free. Besides, I'm not very trusting."

"I'm probably too trusting," she said with a sheepish smile. "Some people say that trust is something that has to be earned. I disagree. I think that trust should be given freely until a person proves unworthy."

"Hmm. That's interesting," Tyler said as he moved next to her on the seat.

"What are you doing?"

Her breathing grew erratic as he put his hand on her leg.

"I'm going to kiss you now."

CHAPTER TWO

ELENA WAS PARALYZED. This was Tyler Knight, her childhood love, who was touching her. And she was incapable of pulling away from him.

His lips met up with hers and she was lost. This was her fantasy come true. No other male had ever stacked up to Tyler. But even Tyler hadn't stacked up to her old idea of him. He'd gone from being her best friend, her lifeline when her father had left her, to being another guy who'd left her, just like her father had.

Now he was back. And he was kissing her. Was that good? It sure as hell — and hell might be the operative word — felt good. His tongue traced her lips, and she sighed against his mouth. And then he burned her up. She'd been kissed before, but never like this. Her body was on fire.

"You're so responsive, baby," he groaned as he pulled her onto his lap, her legs straddling him. Heat pooled inside her as he began undoing her coat.

She should stop this from happening. But as her coat parted and then he pushed it off her shoulders, she couldn't seem to say anything. No sound came from her lips except inarticulate cries of pleasure.

Tyler pushed up against the silk of her panties, and his hardness both frightened and excited her. Maybe he did know who she was; maybe he remembered. Maybe he … she couldn't think anymore.

His lips trailed down her neck and then his fingers were on the front buttons of her uniform, parting it slowly as his lips followed.

"Why were you hiding these, darling?" he said in appreciation as his tongue grazed across the top of her chest.

With way too much familiarity, he unclasped the front of her bra and then filled his hands with her aching breasts. His lips followed as he cupped them and then sucked first one hard nipple and then the other into his warm mouth.

Elena pushed against him. She'd never wanted a man so much. She'd actually never wanted any other man at all. Yet she knew that this was wrong, and she knew she should stop it. But she couldn't.

His mouth skimmed back up her neck and then he was kissing her again while reaching in and sliding his fingers inside her panties.

"You're so wet, baby. Do you want me?" he growled against her lips.

She didn't know how to respond. It was more than obvious that she did. Still, she knew this should stop. She had to tell him she was a virgin. Didn't it hurt the first time a woman had sex?

Before she could speak, Tyler answered his own question. "Yes, you do. It's okay to be a little shy. I'll take care of you. I'll take care of everything."

And then she was moving. He lifted her from his lap and spread her out along the seat. He now lay on top of her and pulled up her leg so he was inside the cradle of her thighs.

He pushed against her while his lips devoured hers and his hands moved up and down her body. With a hard yank, he ripped her panties off, and then he was pressing forward again.

Her wet heat was brushing against the denim of his jeans and the friction was making her crazy. He kissed down her neck again and then feasted on her breasts, making her wriggle beneath him as her body grew tense.

"Mmm, let's see how you taste."

Before she could stop him, he scooted down, lifted her skirt and then his mouth was caressing her womanhood. No man had ever done this, and Elena was now wondering why.

Tyler ran his tongue along her folds and then sucked on her pulsing bud. Then he inserted two fingers inside her and pumped them. Something inside her shattered as pleasure beyond anything imaginable rushed through her.

"Tyler," she cried out.

He continued licking her womanhood in slow, steady strokes, and she floated back down to reality. Then he moved back up her body.

She could only see the outline of his face in the dim lights of the limo, but she didn't care. This was the most miraculous moment of her life. Her night had gone from horrible to exceptional in a matter of minutes.

"I want you so much," he groaned.

He lifted up and tugged down his pants, and then she heard the ripping of foil before he was settling back between her thighs.

"Yes," she sighed as she felt the tip of him pushing inside her heat.

Sensations were already building back up as he leaned down and kissed her on the lips again, his mouth hungry and tasting like sex.

Then he pushed forward, sinking fully inside her with a hard thrust. Elena tensed as a sharp pain erupted inside her. She'd been warned about this. She just hadn't known it would hurt so much.

"Are you okay?" Tyler panted as he moved back and then sank inside her again.

He moved slowly, in and out, and the pain was overrun by a feeling of building pleasure.

"Yes," she sighed.

Everything was okay now.

Tyler leaned down, his hand gripping her breast, his mouth worshipping her neck and his arousal plunging in and out of her. He sped up and she felt unbelievable sensations building within.

"Yes, yes, yes," she chanted, throwing her head back as he squeezed her nipples with ardent fingers.

"That's right baby, feel it," he cried as he pumped even harder.

And then Elena exploded. The first orgasm had been nearly mind-numbing. This time she saw stars behind her eyes as her entire body surged with feeling. Her core pulsed around his amazing manhood, and then he groaned as his body stiffened against her and she felt him pumping his release.

Elena ran her fingers up inside his shirt and stroked his hard, heated skin, feeling utter contentment as he sagged against her.

She'd never thought she would get her best friend back. Until now. This night was magical.

When Tyler pulled away from her, she whimpered, suddenly feeling cold. He sat up and straightened his clothing, and that's when she realized he hadn't taken a single thing off. He'd just shifted his clothes around and gotten down and dirty.

Suddenly struck with embarrassment, she sat up and buttoned up her uniform, then pulled on her coat. She could do nothing about the panties. They were destroyed. She didn't know what to say to him now.

"That was great, darling. Do you need a ride home?"

Tyler's words took a moment to process. "What do you mean?" she finally choked out.

"My buddies are going to come searching for me soon. But I can have our driver give you a ride home before he comes back for us."

Elena's embarrassment morphed into total mortification. She'd just given her virginity to a man who had no clue who she was. He didn't even know her name. He was so drunk that he probably couldn't pick her out of a lineup.

What in the world had she been thinking? Oh, right. She hadn't been thinking.

"No. I have transportation," she said. She needed to get away from this man before he saw her cry.

"Are you sure? You did have a couple of drinks," he said, though he was still opening the door of the limo.

"I'm not driving," she told him.

She followed him out onto the pavement without any assistance from him.

When she stepped outside, the streetlights illuminated his face, a face she'd dreamed about for the past ten years.

"Thanks again, doll. That was great."

He leaned forward and kissed her, a quick kiss. And then he turned around and made his way back inside the gentleman's club.

It took a few moments for Elena's feet to move, and when they did, she felt numb all over. Surprisingly, no tears fell as she walked to the bus, got on and rode the route home. She didn't even cry once she was home.

But when the numbness wore off, rage took its place. If ever there were an opportunity, she would return the favor of making Tyler feel like a used piece of trash. He was obviously destined to burn in hell, and she'd make hell come for him even sooner than anyone expected if she had her way.

CHAPTER THREE

Eight Years Later

"YOU'VE BECOME BORING in your old age."

A remark like that from his best friend? What was the world coming to? Tyler shot the guy a look that no one could interpret as friendly, picked up his drink, and downed the rest before he bothered to reply.

"It's called growing up, Matt. We all have to do it sometime."

"If growing up is so much damn fun, then you can count me out," Matt told him before scanning the room.

"I hardly expected you ever to do such a reasonable thing," Tyler told him. "I know you too well."

"You and I are both only thirty-one, Tyler. It's not as if we have one foot in the grave now."

"There are days I feel like I do, Matt. Work can be draining, all-consuming," Tyler said.

"If you'd let your hair down once in a while, old boy, maybe you wouldn't be so damn miserable. All work and no play makes *you* incredibly dull."

"I can't win, can I? If I go out on the town too much, the papers label me an effing playboy. If I stay out of the tabloids and devote myself to hard work, then I'm a hermit. You can all piss off," Tyler said, holding up his hand for a refill. The freaking bartender should certainly be more on top of his job.

"No one has ever said that life is easy," Matt told him with a laugh. "Why don't you find a girl and take her to your room and fu — oops, I mean make love till the morning light is breaking through the windows?"

"*Make love*? And they say that I'm the romantic one in my clan," Tyler snickered.

"I'm trying to be sophisticated," Matt replied. "After all, we're in a higher-class bar right now."

"And whose damn idea was that?" Tyler said, scanning the room with distaste. A good rowdy pub was far more his style, or at least it had been his style until last year, when he'd decided to try growing up a little bit more. Or to look as if he'd grown up a bit.

Maybe he did need to get laid. It had been a while — way too long. When was the last time he'd had a woman moaning beneath him? That he even had to search his memory told him it was past time to *do* something He needed a good lay, and he wasn't thinking of poetry. Nothing flowery at all. Hell, pin the broad to the mattress and do what nature intended the two of them to do.

He'd once fought with his brothers on a constant basis, telling them that love was real, that it could be achieved, but his last relationship had ended in disaster. Utter disaster. He'd been willing to give the woman a six-carat diamond along with his heart. And then he'd found her in the broom closet at his oldest brother's wedding — with the bellhop.

Byron had pointed out to him that night that women couldn't be trusted. Tyler wasn't ready to go that far, but as far as looking for happily-ever-after… Well, maybe he'd just look for Ms. *Right Now*.

But here was the problem. No one was catching his eye, and he was growing bored with this bar, so he decided to write this night off as a bust. Get real. It was time to hoist himself up off this bar stool and get the eff out of Dodge. But just then he heard the sound of laugher, and something about it caught his attention.

He looked off to the side and couldn't help but noticing right there before him an appealing backside, exposed by a low-slung silky red tank top. Whoa.

"Hmm, maybe tonight will be more interesting than I'd originally thought," Tyler told Matt.

"What makes you think she'll have anything to do with you?" Matt replied, zeroing in on the woman with that fabulous ass, but whose face they couldn't yet see.

"If I want her, she'll be more than willing to have something — more than something — to do with me."

"If only I could be one of the infamous Knight brothers for a day," Matt muttered.

"Shut up, Matt. Don't even pretend you're humble," Tyler told his friend, still gazing at the woman, not wanting to miss the moment when she turned around. After all, she could be a dog.

"Compared with you and your brothers, I'm a damn saint," Matt said, the smile obvious in his voice.

"Maybe so, but I'm the nice guy of the three of us Knights," Tyler told him.

Matt had to laugh. "The sad thing about that statement is that it's true," he muttered.

"When you're raised by narcissistic parents — to use a fancy psychological term — parents who then get murdered before your eyes, it tends to make you a little bit ... shall we say, aloof," Tyler replied.

"Then how have you always been able to stay so positive?"

"I don't know. I was so young when it happened. My brothers got the worst end of that stick. I guess I just feel that life is too short to dwell in the past. My philosophy is that a night in the arms of the right woman can heal the most wounded of souls."

"Then why haven't you bedded anyone lately?" Matt asked.

"How the hell do you know that I haven't?" Tyler grumbled.

"You've been complaining about it for a while," Matt pointed out.

"Yeah, I need to learn to keep my damn mouth shut."

"So why not settle down?"

" I was ready to and I failed epically. How in hell did I make such a bad choice in a woman? I don't know, man. I think it's harder than people realize to find that one woman you can't live without. I love women, love how they feel, how they smell, how they ... taste. Then their true colors come out, and their claws sharpen. If I could find that girl without a hidden agenda or a tendency to fuck strangers in a closet, then maybe, just maybe, I would do exactly that — settle down."

"Damn, Tyler. Should I call up Oprah now?"

"Go to hell, Matt. Maybe my future wife is right over there in a very appealing red tank top," Tyler said as he stood up.

"Well, then, go and get her, tiger." Matt signaled for the bill.

The woman finally turned, and when she looked up, her eyes met with Tyler's across the room, and he felt as if he'd been punched in the stomach.

"Who in the hell is she?" he whispered, though he wasn't looking for a response.

"Holy shit, she's gorgeous," Matt muttered. "There's no way that woman is available."

Just then she lifted a delicate hand and brushed back her sun-kissed golden brown hair, the thick strands falling over her shoulders and hanging midway down her back. The bar was dim, but even from about twenty feet away, Tyler could see that she had light eyes, shining eyes, and her lips — damn, her lips were plump and pink, and they were calling to him.

Tyler didn't give a flying whatever if the woman was taken. He knew for sure he wasn't leaving this bar without her.

CHAPTER FOUR

"DO YOU KNOW the man who's looking at you like you're dessert?"

It took several moments for Elena to realize that her friend Piper had spoken to her, because, yes, she did know exactly who was looking at her. And her gaze was fully captured by the one and only Tyler Knight.

"Hello? Earth to Elena," Piper said, and she laughed as she bumped into her.

Finally, Elena was able to break eye contact with Tyler, and she looked back toward her friend, feeling slightly dazed.

"Yes … um … yes, I know who he is," Elena said as she lifted her drink and took a long swallow.

"Do you care to share?" Piper asked with no little impatience.

Shaking off the shock of seeing the man who had once been her best friend, and then who had humiliated her almost beyond repair ten years later, Elena was consumed with anger. How dare this worthless bastard look at her now as if he wanted to devour her?

A lot had changed since the last time she'd seen Tyler. She'd gone from gangly to womanly, with more curves than she cared to have She'd also decided that she enjoyed wearing a little makeup, and that she really enjoyed doing her hair, but even with those changes, she was still the same person on the inside.

She was still Elena Truman, and she still suffered from insecurity — hell, insecurities, plural — when it came to men.

"Okay, let me rephrase this," Piper said, placing her hands on Elena's shoulders and shaking them to get her friend's attention. "You *will* tell me who he is!"

"He was my best friend when we were children — until he realized he was too cool to play with a mere girl anymore. Then, when I was in college and working …" She trailed off. This wasn't something she wanted to talk about.

"You mean when you were going through your geeky phase?" Piper asked.

"Thanks for being so supportive," Elena said through gritted teeth.

"Just tell me what happened and I'll be nice."

"There's no time," Elena told her. "It looks like he's going to walk over. Maybe it's my turn for a little revenge. Why should he get away with being a complete douche without suffering any consequences?" Hey. She really liked this idea. Was it just the booze talking?

"I don't know, Elena. Revenge never ends well." Piper swiveled around and saw that Tyler did seem to be planning to head their way.

"For the loser it doesn't," Elena said. "It's all a matter of perspective. Just have my back."

"I don't know," Piper replied. "You're acting a little crazy right now."

"I'm fine. I just wasn't expecting to see him ever again — that's all," Elena told her before taking another gulp of liquid courage.

"I think you've had enough to drink. Elena. I also think you should abort this mission right now."

"I'm fine. I promise you," Elena said. She gave her friend a determined look, but she put the drink down on the table.

"Look, Elena, it's been a lot of years since you've seen this guy, right? Let's try to think through this. Maybe he isn't the monster he once was. People change." Piper peeked back across the bar. "But you'd better make a decision, and fast."

"The panic in your voice isn't helping me right now, Piper. And don't let his looks or his charm deceive you. Tyler Knight does what he wants when he wants, and he doesn't give a damn about who gets hurt in the process. There's no way that he's changed."

"What in the hell happened!"

"Stop talking about it. He's almost here. Go to the bar and flirt with the bartender, and most importantly, have faith in your best friend," Elena whispered frantically.

"I'll be watching." With that Piper walked away.

Elena only had a moment to compose her features before she felt Tyler behind her. She didn't even need to turn to know he was there. Damn, the man had been blessed with more charisma than any one person deserved. It just wasn't right.

He'd had it even back when they were kids, and later in life, when she'd been gangly and he'd been perfection in the back seat of a limo. She just hadn't realized how little, how dismissively, he thought of women. It hadn't taken her too many years in the scheme of things to figure it out — or to blossom from the long-legged, too skinny, dirt-faced young tomboy she'd been.

She hadn't spoken to Tyler in eight years. This reunion was long overdue, and her dislike of him had grown fierce with time. After he had rejected her early on, his meanness hadn't been good enough. No, he'd had to then come into her life once more and humiliate her, take her virginity and then treat her like a whore. In theory, she'd been a woman for two years by then, but she'd been shy and awkward, little more than a girl, really, and he'd made it so much worse. Just her luck.

Well, this time, Tyler would be the one to feel something other than smugness. He could feel what it was like to be humiliated and left wanting something that he couldn't have.

"Good evening."

Even the sound of his voice right behind her ear sent shivers traveling through her body. This wasn't going to be as easy as she'd envisioned just a minute before. But Elena wasn't a quitter. Never had been, and never would be. This was a battle she would most certainly win.

"Are you speaking to me?" She turned around slowly, her eyelids lowered just the slightest bit, her lips in a perfect pout.

A femme fatale was so not like her. But anyone with a little bit of gumption and a whole lot of will could pull this act off if she tried hard enough. And she was more than ready to try.

"Would you like to dance?" he asked.

"Excuse me, but do I know you?" She licked her bottom lip so his eyes were drawn there.

"We'll get to know each other while we dance," he said, holding out his hand.

"I don't think so," she said, leaning back against the high table next to her.

His eyes narrowed and something almost predatory leapt into them before he next spoke. "I don't play games."

With that said, he moved forward, invading her personal space. She wanted to take a step back — all she could do now was breathe his scent

— but a seductress would never do that, so she thrust her chin out and moved an inch closer to him.

"Neither do I," she practically purred, hating herself just the tiniest bit for doing it.

"Good. Because I would like to dance with you," he said before grinning. "And then I'd like to take you home."

Elena was too stunned for a moment to respond. She'd expected boldness from him after her last encounter, but she hadn't expected him to be this upfront about his intentions. What she wanted to do was slap him across his smug face. She barely restrained herself from doing just that.

"Well, how very subtle of you," she said with a tinkling laugh. "And what makes you think for even a moment that I'm the type of girl who would take you up on an offer like that?"

"We made a connection, even in a room full of other people. Don't tell me that you didn't feel it."

"Oh, believe me, I felt it," she said, lifting her hand and tracing a perfectly manicured fingernail down his arm. "But I have some standards, sad to say. Here's one of them — I don't go home with strangers in the night, particularly ones I meet in a bar."

"And I told you that I don't play games," he said, moving yet another inch closer. Her breasts were brushing against his impressively hard chest.

A shudder rushed through her and she knew she was out of her league. She thought for a moment of crying mercy and bailing out on this impromptu mission, but then he lifted his eyebrow just the way he had the last time he'd rejected her, and she knew she wasn't going anywhere. But she knew something about gamesmanship. In fact, she had a degree in it.

"Fine. Walk away, then," she told him with a careless shrug.

She turned back to the table and lifted her drink. If he called her bluff and left, then good riddance, but everything inside her was saying that he wasn't going anywhere.

When he brushed up against her back, his hands closing over her shoulders, she knew she had him, hook, line, and sinker. She'd never felt anything quite like this. The power of knowing that for once he was in *her* power.

"You're making me break my rules," he said, his breath whispering across her ear before he turned her around to face him again. "Tell me your name."

That was an improvement. He wasn't treating her quite like a piece of meat now.

"Do you always talk as if you're commanding people?"

"I can be laid-back. But not quite yet. And when I want something, I go for it. Tell me your name."

She smiled, this time a real smile, and his eyes dilated, making the butterflies in her stomach take flight. "You tell me your name first," she said, her voice just a little too breathless, and she didn't need any acting skills to achieve that effect just now.

"Tyler." He didn't add anything. He just waited.

"Elena," she finally said. There was no recognition in his eyes. Of course, he'd always called her Lanie when they were younger. But why would she think for even a moment that he would remember her? She was just one more castoff in his life, one of a long line of castoffs.

"Got a last name, Elena?" he said after a few moments of silence.

"My last name has to be earned," she told him.

It took a moment, but then his face was transformed. His lips turned up first in a wide smile, and then he laughed. A deep-in-the-gut happy laughter that had her own lips turning up.

"I think I could like you, Elena. Let me buy you a drink," he said. Without waiting for a yes or a no, he held up a hand, and a waitress came over.

"I guarantee that you'll like me, Tyler."

"I guess I'm going to have to break another one of my rules, then," he said as he boxed her in even further.

She waited, but when he didn't elaborate, she asked, "And what rule is that, Tyler?"

The smoldering look he sent her had her entire body responding to the man, fully against her will. Then he leaned forward as if he were about to impart a great secret.

"Let the games begin."

He said no more, and Elena could almost hear the dinging of a bell as round one got underway.

"I thought you said that you didn't play games."

"As I said, I'm breaking one of my rules. And all in your honor."

Ah. So he was telling her he was more than ready to play with her. True to his usual type.

"Yes, Tyler, let the games begin."

CHAPTER FIVE

THERE WAS SOMETHING so familiar about this woman. But Tyler had been sitting there in the bar with her for over an hour, and he just couldn't place her, so it all had to be an illusion. Elena wasn't the type of woman a man could forget. She was certainly a woman a man broke the rules for, though.

Tyler could easily walk away from most of the females who crossed his path. Yes, he sometimes spoke of marriage and babies and growing up, but the idea of doing that in reality terrified him to the very depths of his soul. He still had that diamond ring, as a reminder of his near escape. And he was a lot more guarded now.

He always came on strong. Why not? He was great-looking, rich as sin, and had what one ex had referred to as the *ultimate swagger*. Tyler knew he was a catch. Most of the time, he didn't have to break a sweat to get a hot babe into bed.

So why had it seemed crucial to his very existence that he stay and talk to this woman, a woman who clearly had some sort of agenda? He had no clue what that agenda was, but he could see a mile away when someone who was playing a game. Elena had secrets, but they were ones that Tyler wanted to figure out. Most certainly. Was she after money?

Fame in the tabloids, maybe to help her jump-start a modeling career? Or was there something deeper? Darker? More sinister?

The idea — the uncertainty — should terrify him. Instead, he was more turned on than ever before.

He should have just blown her off, but something about her made him willing to play along, willing to almost get down on his knees and beg her to let him just stay in her presence. He was heading down a dangerous road, and yet he couldn't seem to look for an exit.

"Are you seeing anyone, Elena?"

He watched her reaction. And his question didn't make her jumpy in the least.

"Not at the moment. I like my freedom," she told him. "What about you? Any girlfriends about to come out of the restroom and fight me for the privilege of seeing you?"

She had such quick comebacks, and he loved them. "I can't guarantee that won't happen," Tyler replied.

"Then maybe I should change seats," she said.

"Are you afraid of a challenge, Elena? You don't strike me as the type of girl to run from a fight."

"Oh, I'm not afraid of any woman you most likely take out on dates. Let me guess. They're the stick-thin Barbie doll types with bigger bust sizes than brains." Elena said this all so casually that it took him a moment to realize she was insulting him.

"Then what am I doing sitting here talking to you? Your bust size is respectable, of course. But are you a ditzy sort of girl?"

She laughed openly at that. "*Ditzy!* Nice word, and especially used with *girl*, it pegs you as a retrograde. I have a college degree — maybe more than one. I don't think I could be called stupid."

"It depends what level and what area the degree is in," he countered.

"You haven't earned that information yet."

"That's the second time you've made that comment. You're incredibly good at dodging any kind of question about yourself. Is that on purpose, or are you running on automatic?"

She looked down for a moment, and Tyler instantly reached across the small table and lifted her chin. He couldn't read her if he couldn't see into her eyes. That wouldn't work for him.

"I don't know you enough to let you inside my head, Tyler. Has anyone ever told you that you're too damn pushy?" She shook off his hand.

"I've been told that a lot. But the thing is," he said before leaning back, that appealing crooked grin on his lips, "I always get what I want — one way or another."

"Maybe not this time," she said, and he saw a flash in her eyes that he couldn't quite interpret. Fascinating.

This witch, this foxy lady, had him even more intrigued than before. Tyler had to know her story. And he would.

His body was humming with lust, but even more than that, he was actually interested in this mystery woman. She somehow compelled him, and she made him want to trust her. That was insane. She was playing him — he knew that beyond a shadow of a doubt. But what could he do but go along? She had him by the short hairs.

He had to reply somehow, so he came out with this. "Tell me something real about yourself."

"I've been telling you things about me for the past hour," she told him.

"No, Elena. You've been holding me on a fishing line just enough to keep me hooked, but not enough to reel me in. Tell me something real."

She froze and her eyes flew open with something like shock, but she managed to mask her expression in an instant. She was good at that.

"You tell me something *real* about yourself first, and then I'll do the same," she said.

Tyler laughed again. He'd found himself doing that a lot in the last hour. Another interesting thing in Elena's favor.

"Fine," he told her. "I have nothing to hide." He thought for a moment and then grinned. "I've never slept with a woman."

Her mouth dropped open, but after a few moments, she sent him a withering look.

"If you honestly think I'll believe that, then you are about the stupidest man I've ever met."

"It's a fact."

"Really?" Her words dripped with scorn. "You come over to me and tell me you want to take me over to your — what? bachelor pad? — but you've never done that before?"

Man, was he enjoying himself, and he couldn't help but smile. His buddy Matt was definitely going to have to get another ride, because one way or the other Tyler was taking Elena home with him.

"I've certainly done that before. I've just never slept with a woman."

Her glare turned to confusion. And he wasn't going to help her figure out what he'd just said. He wanted to see how smart she really was.

"Ah, so you're the dine-and-dash sort of guy?" she finally said.

"No. I always treat my women with the utmost respect. We do what we do together for the same reason — to feel good."

"That's so admirable. But you screw them and then leave immediately. I bet you have all sorts of hotel rooms on standby just for these *special* occasions."

"I wouldn't characterize myself quite that way, but I do like a good night's sleep. Alone," he said before leaning closer. "And yet I have a feeling you might change my mind about that."

There was no need to talk about his last long-term relationship. No, he'd never slept over at that woman's place, and she had never slept over at his, but that was mostly due to work schedules, and he must have known then that something wasn't quite right.

Elena was silent for several heartbeats before she threw him a smile, and she leaned toward him, their faces now only a couple of inches apart.

"I guarantee you that if we were in bed together, even if you managed to stick around for a whole night, you'd have a good night, but not much sleep," she said in a throaty purr that went straight to his groin and left him aching in a way he hadn't ached since high school.

"Prove it."

CHAPTER SIX

ELENA TOOK LONG, deep breaths in front of the restroom mirror. She was in a major battle to get her heart to quit racing. Those words, those exact words he'd spoken to her eighteen years before, had been too much for her to handle.

She'd been unable to speak. She'd just lurched up from the table and run.

"What's wrong? What happened? Are you okay? Let me get you a washcloth."

Her friend Piper had rushed through the door and was talking a mile a minute and not giving Elena a chance to answer. But Elena couldn't answer yet anyway. She was too frazzled.

Piper handed her a cool cloth, and Elena pressed it to her forehead.

"Okay, I'm giving you exactly sixty seconds to pull yourself together and to tell me what in the hell is going on. If I need to go and kick that guy's ass, I'm your girl. I'm officially a brown belt in karate now."

The fact that Piper was deadly serious yanked Elena's mood around. For a moment she just starred at Piper in surprise. Then she broke out into a broad smile and began laughing uncontrollably.

"I'm starting to get really worried now, Elena. Seriously. If you don't stop laughing and talk to me, I'm going to have to call in the paramedics," Piper said, folding her arms across her chest and tapping her foot impatiently. "Or maybe the guys who will fit you with a straitjacket."

"I'm so … so sorry Piper. It's just that you are the best friend that any girl could ever have, and I love you so much. Thank you," Elena said between fits of guffawing.

"Yeah, yeah, you're my bestie too," Piper snapped. "Now, tell me what is going on! I mean it, Elena. I'm serious!"

"Okay, okay. It's just that things are going just fine. I know he wants me, wants me desperately, which is pretty great, actually — all things considered — but then the ass tells me to *prove it* and I just lost it and headed for the hills."

Piper looked at her friend in complete puzzlement. Yes, she wanted Elena's story. But as a true bestie would do, she didn't care what Tyler had done. She was ready to kill him just because Elena wanted to.

"It's settled," Piper said. "I'm going to kick his ass because he's upset you." She made one hand into a fist and smacked the other one with it.

"No. Don't do that," Elena said, overcome with a fit of giggles again. "You've done exactly what I needed you to do. I needed a minute to calm down. I have to end the evening on the proper note. With the proper touch. Or maybe a not-so-proper touch."

Her friend looked at her dubiously. "Then we're leaving?"

"In a few minutes," Elena told her, and Piper threw up her hands. "I'm going to go back out there, sweetie, so I can get him hot and bothered, and then I'll leave him wanting more. I need you to come out of the bathroom in exactly five minutes and tell me that it's time to go. Then we'll talk more. I promise."

"I don't like this, Elena. I don't like it at all. And you're going to tell me exactly what this asshat has done."

"I know you don't like it, but because we will do anything for each other, you'll carry through with my crazy plans," Elena said before checking herself out in the mirror. "And I promise to tell you all. You're going to kill me, though, for not telling you sooner."

She looked slightly crazy, but then she was feeling a little bit crazy at the moment. She was certifiably insane, actually, to think she could carry this off. Yes, bring on that straitjacket. But she was doing it, and she was doing it well — so far, at least. She was no longer a clueless twenty-year-old who could be used and tossed away like trash.

"Fine. You have exactly five minutes," Piper warned her, and she plopped down on one of the benches in front of the full-length mirrors.

"Thanks. Love you tons."

With that, Elena walked steadily ahead, took another deep breath, and swung the door open. When she turned the corner of the short hallway, she found Tyler leaning against the wall. His expression was unreadable, but that was fine by her. She could wear a pretty damn good mask of her own, if she had to say so.

"Are you okay, Elena?"

That was all he said.

"I'm sorry. My drink hit me wrong and I got overheated — hot *all* over. I had to cool down," she said as she slinked up to him. His eyes widened when she put out a hand and caressed his chest. "I believe you told me to *prove it*."

And then she leaned against him, circling her hand behind his head and pulling him down to her. She captured his lips and opened herself up, her hands splaying across his chest, her tongue tasting his excitement.

Tyler's shock at her boldness lasted only a second, maybe less, and then he was pinning her against the wall as his mouth devoured hers.

Elena had been prepared for the kiss, or at least she'd thought she'd been prepared. But as his tongue traced the contours of her mouth, her stomach tightened and her core grew dangerously wet. And she knew that no amount of preparation in the world could have clued her in to how good it would feel to be in his arms again, even if she hated the man.

His body was hard and unyielding, and he was running his hands up and down her sides, drawing closer and closer to her breasts with each pass. What he was doing with his mouth — she'd never experienced anything like it before.

His touch was searing her, and when a low groan erupted from his throat, the sound traveled straight through her veins and pulsed deep inside. No, she hadn't thought this revenge plot through. Not at all.

"Oh, Elena, are you as turned on as I am right now?" He leaned back only far enough to trail his lips across her jaw and trace the skin at her neck.

"I … uh … we … Too pubic … public!" she stuttered, her embarrassment quickly forgotten, although her hunger had been so exposed. Her desperate fingers were clasping his shoulders, holding him to her. She was trying to stop, but her body was rebelling.

"No one is back here," he said. He slipped his hand beneath her shirt and stroked her now quivering stomach.

When he reached the underside of her breasts, she held her breath. She should call a halt right now. This wasn't part of her plan, but she waited, instead, for what was coming next. She was aching for this.

He didn't disappoint her. His hand traced over the lacy fabric of her bra, and his palm cupped her jutting nipples, making her moan in pleasure.

"You like my touch, don't you, Elena?" he said. He sucked her bottom lip into his mouth and bit down gently. "Yes, I can feel how much you do," he answered for her. "Forget about dancing here. Let's go back to my place, and we can really dance."

She was trying to remember why she couldn't do that, why she had to say no.

"Um, Elena ... Hello!"

Elena heard her name, knew it wasn't Tyler speaking, but for the life of her she couldn't drag herself out of the sexual fog that was surrounding her.

"Go away. Elena's busy," she heard Tyler growl.

"I don't think so," Piper grated out.

"Piper!" Her friend's irritated voice brought Elena back to reality, and she managed to push, rather than pull, against Tyler's chest.

That was all it took for him to take a step back.

"I'm ready to leave now," Piper said, sending a meaningful look Elena's way, reminding her that this was what she'd asked her to do five minutes ago.

Five minutes ago seemed liked eons.

"I'm sorry. Yes, it's time to go," Elena said. She hoped no one noticed that she was panting.

"Don't," Tyler said, almost a panic in his eyes. "I'll take you home later."

Elena was oh so tempted, but she needed to pull herself together. If she went home with this guy tonight, she would be the one losing. Yet again.

"Sorry, Tyler," she said, the purr back in her voice for a third time. "I have to leave now."

After walking a couple of steps away, she whirled back around and pulled a piece of paper and pen from her purse, jotted down her number, and moved back over to him. She slipped it right there into the front pocket of his trousers, and she let her hand linger there, so close to where she knew he was the hardest. Damn, how she wanted to touch him. *Touch* wasn't the word she was really thinking, of course.

"You may call me," she said with just enough sass that she watched a spark light his eyes.

She didn't look back at him again. She took her friend's arm and walked away, and she didn't breathe until they were outside in the fresh air.

"You are *so* spilling," Piper growled as she hailed a cab and they slipped inside.

"I will. I promise," Elena replied, leaning her head back against the vinyl headrest. "Just not yet. For now, I'm going to close my eyes and try to get my body under control."

"You're in trouble, Elena, big trouble. If you carry through with this, I don't think Tyler Knight is going to be the one who gets punished."

"Yeah, I know that too," Elena said.

And then she was done talking. Her friend was right. She was in trouble — big, huge, monstrous trouble.

CHAPTER SEVEN

THE DAY WAS warm, exceptionally warm for May in Seattle. Elena had changed her mind several times in the hour before finally going to meet Tyler. How was she supposed to make him want her so badly that it would kill him to lose her if she kept refusing to see him?

He'd called her before she'd even made it home after the night at the club, and then he'd continued calling her all week. She'd put him off long enough.

Now she found herself next to his car as he tugged on the tie he was wearing.

"I think I overdressed," he told her, the knot slipping loose and the satin sliding through his fingers.

Elena found her focus drifting to his chest, and then chastised herself for her ridiculous hormones. She didn't desire him — okay, she didn't want to desire him.

"I should have checked the weather before leaving the apartment," she said, wishing that she'd worn a T-shirt instead of a sweater. She didn't have anything beneath the damnable sweater, so she was most likely going to suffer.

"Climb inside," he told her. "We're running late."

"Where are we going?"

"One of my favorite places. It's outside the city and quiet."

That didn't answer her question, but she found herself sitting down and buckling up, and soon they were on their way.

Elena wasn't sure if it was the heat or the man sitting next to her, but she couldn't get comfortable. After they rode in silence for about half an hour, he was approaching one of the ports.

"Are we taking a ferry?"

"Yes."

They didn't have to wait long until they were given the go-ahead to drive onto the ferry, and then Tyler turned toward her as other passengers exited their cars and moved toward the stairs. Everyone else was eager to sit out on the deck as the boat made its way to one of the islands near Seattle.

As he looked into her eyes, Elena knew right then and there that she was making a very foolish mistake. After she made love to Tyler eight years ago — well, to be realistic he'd used her like a cheap hooker — she'd been devastated. The man still didn't remember her, yet her body was in a constant state of arousal around him.

She should stop with these plans of hers, get out of his car, get back to the shore, and find her way home. What she shouldn't be doing was sitting in a hot car with this even hotter man, breathing in his scent, gazing at what could only be described as perfection.

"I really have a lot of work to do this weekend, so I don't want to be out late," she told him.

"Really? What kind of work?"

She froze. He didn't know she was an attorney, didn't know anything about what she did. That's how she wanted to keep it. The less he knew about her, the better.

"I don't want to get into all the boring details," she said with a false laugh. "Besides, if I start telling you about my work, we won't have any mystery left between us."

"I like mystery, but not lies, sweetheart," he said, and she shifted in her seat. "I spoke to Piper last night when I wasn't able to get ahold of you, and she said you 'girls' didn't have any plans this weekend, that you were planning on watching a bunch of movies and eating gallons of ice cream."

"Piper told you this?" Elena was horrified.

"It took some prying, but I'm good at obtaining information."

"And this is something that gives you a sense of satisfaction?"

"Very," he told her. "I can see that you disagree, but in the business world, you obtain information on your opponents. It's how you stay on top."

Elena felt her heart slowing as her irritation grew. Her infatuation with the man diminished markedly when he was ticking her off.

"So you think it's okay to invade a person's privacy?"

If she hadn't been so annoyed, she might have thought her words through. This wasn't the way to seduce any man, and especially a playboy like Tyler. But it was hard to keep her eye on the end of the game when the guy sitting next to her caused so many conflicting emotions to roll through her in such a short amount of time.

"If necessary."

"Am I your opponent, Tyler?"

"No, Elena. You are a challenge. I never give up on a challenge."

"You're so smooth, Tyler. You always seem to know exactly what to say, don't you?"

He was so much more sophisticated than she was. The chances of her winning even this round were slim to none in reality. Wouldn't she be far wiser just to go back home, and do it pronto?

"I'd say that's an accurate description of me."

"And it doesn't bother you if people might not find any merit to your words? After all, you apparently spew them out without any serious thought."

That made him pause for a moment.

"You don't mince words, do you, Elena?"

"No," she told him. "Granted, I can do it in style. I'm capable of making mincemeat out of anyone or anything." Eek. Was she getting too close to the fact that she was a lawyer? "But in general, I find honesty to be best way to go." Okay, so she was being a bit ironic, but what could she say?

"I do as well. So, in all fairness, I should warn you that I plan on sharing a bed with you very soon."

Elena's heart rate hit into overdrive again, just like that. He reached across and placed his hand on her leg. She wanted to push him away, to tell him there was no way in hell that was going to happen, but she stopped herself at the last minute.

"I think that you suggested something like that back when we first met. If — and that's a big *if* — I decide that you might be someone worthy of 'sharing a bed' with," she said, her voice husky. She wasn't even acting when the breathlessness crept in once again. Dammit.

"Believe me, you'll find me worthy. And more than 'a *big if*.' You'll never want to leave once I've sunk inside you."

Clenching her jaw to keep from groaning, she felt her body tense. But it was absurd. Why was she feeling the heat? And why was she fighting an image of the two of them sweaty and entwined? It was flashing through her mind, and she hated herself for that.

"Does that come from *long* experience, Tyler? Or have your multiple partners left a thank-you note beside the bed telling you how incredible you are?"

Tyler didn't even blink. He grabbed her hand and brought it to his lips, kissed her knuckles, and brushed his tongue across her palm in a slow caress.

"I know myself, Elena. I know what I want and I know when a woman wants me. And, darling, you want me as much as I want you. I'm willing to jump through some hoops to make it to your bed. I have faith that you will be worth the wait."

Faith? That was an odd word to use. But molten heat settled between her thighs as he continued kissing her hand and wrist. She tugged, but he wasn't letting her go. If she fought him too hard, this was over. But if she continued letting him kiss her the way he was, she was going to melt into a puddle. She was more than wet as it was.

When the horn sounded, alerting them that they were pulling up to the port, she breathed a sigh of relief. If she'd had to deal with more of his tongue and lips on her skin, she'd have been begging him to climb into the backseat of his SUV.

Yes, a backseat. That brought back old memories of Tyler Knight. Though this backseat was smaller than the one she'd lost her virginity in.

"Saved by the bell," he told her as the traffic began moving forward. "For now."

"Are you going to tell me yet where we're going?"

The island he had chosen was a favorite place of hers, small, quiet, intimate, though he didn't know that. Now she would remember being there with him and her memories would be tainted.

"I have a cabin here. I thought we'd do a late lunch," he said with a smile. "And if we choose, we can stay the night."

"That won't happen," Elena told him, panic tightening her throat.

"We'll just have to see how it goes. I'm optimistic, and I have good reason for that."

The seductive smile he sent her had her body trembling. She could handle him, but could she handle herself?

CHAPTER EIGHT

TYLER FELT AS if he were walking in a field of land mines. But if he didn't show his fear to Elena, he might be able to avoid an explosion. Never let them see you sweat, and pray for the best, and all those old, hackneyed lines. But the tactic had worked for him so far, and maybe it would again.

For a week he'd been playing phone tag with this woman. Under normal circumstances, he would have bailed out after the first day. He knew when someone wasn't telling the whole truth, and Elena sure as hell wasn't.

What was she hiding? He didn't have a clue. She probably knew exactly who he was and she was hoping to entrap him. Broken condom? Faked pregnancy? Who knew? But he'd already had a couple of disastrous relationships and there was no chance of that happening again.

Still, there was something about this woman — something so familiar. It was almost as if he knew her, but that wasn't possible. He'd already gone over that in his brain before. Maybe the whole thing was just elemental. He had to have her, had to see this thing through to its inevitable conclusion.

He would have her in his bed. And then he'd be done with her. No problem. No pain. And who wanted any gain?

As he pulled up to his cabin, he wondered why he was bringing her to this place. It was his retreat, a place he and his brothers all came to when they wanted to get away from the city, away from the chaos of their lives. They didn't bring women there.

"I wasn't expecting this," Elena said, breaking him from his reverie.

The water gently lapping at the shore and the birds singing in the trees were the only sounds that could be heard, and the nearest neighbor was a mile down the road. This was one of his favorite places in the whole wide world. Jeez. Why was he always reverting to clichés nowadays? *Get a grip, man.*

And he did. "I enjoy the quiet when I come up here. There aren't a lot of people around, and we count everyone in the area as friends. We also respect one another's privacy."

He opened the car door on his side before she could respond, and he felt a smidgen of frustration when she didn't wait for him to come around to assist her before she started to get out of her side. He still waited as she climbed out, and he made a point of shutting her door, though he hadn't been able to do the chivalrous thing and open it.

This certainly wasn't something his parents had taught him. No. It had been taught to him by Bill, the man who'd raised him, the man who had given him values. Tyler had turned his nose up at those values for a few selfish years, but he'd gotten past that, hadn't he?

He wasn't proud of that time in his life, that time when he'd been drinking too much, made no real friendships, and had turned his nose up at the people in his life who mattered most. Bill had been greatly relieved when Tyler had pulled his head out of his ass.

Tyler had served his time. He'd done penance, or so he hoped.

"I've always enjoyed these islands," Elena said. "They've grown more crowded over the years, but you can still find quiet places. Thanks for bringing me here."

Tyler was surprised by her genuine enthusiasm for a place he loved. He was so on guard with the woman that he could almost discern her game-playing versus her moments of genuineness.

Once they were inside the living room, he watched Elena as she looked at the pictures hung on the walls and the simple pieces of oak and leather furniture. The home was comfortable with a fireplace, nice stereo system, and plush furnishings. It certainly wasn't lavish.

"No TV?" she asked.

"Nope. All of us come here to get away from that sort of noise," he told her. "We do, however, enjoy having music. We also have Internet.

None of us can get away from that for even a single day. We start going into withdrawal — the shakes and pink elephants and all that."

She stepped outside the back door with him behind her, and the weathered wooden boards creaked beneath their feet. The air was cooler over here than it had been in the city, which made it a perfect time to start a little fire.

He left her alone while he gathered the wood and put it together in the rock fire pit he'd had specially built.

"I hope you enjoy barbecue," he told her after the blaze was going strong, and he dragged out a couple of chairs.

"I'm no vegan, though some of my best friends are. My tastes are fairly wide-ranging, and I definitely like a good piece of meat."

The hungry look she sent his way had his groin tightening. She confused him. One moment she was sending him all the right signals, and the next she was putting on a chastity belt.

Without a second thought, he grabbed her, tugging her tightly into his arms. "Dessert should always come first," he murmured.

His lips fastened to hers and he didn't waste time gaining full access to her mouth. With a groan, he feasted on her, reveling in their first kiss since that night at the bar.

When he pulled back, Tyler wasn't sure what he'd been expecting — if he'd been thinking the passion between them was nothing but a fluke or not. But it was so much more powerful than he'd remembered.

He needed this woman. Had to have her.

"I'll start our lunch."

He left her on the back patio before going inside and gathering the steaks he'd had brought in. The next half hour stabilized him. He loved cooking, and the routine of it eased the ever-pulsing need for her that was racking his body.

He and Elena chatted while the steak cooked and rested, and he put together a salad and warmed bread. He'd have preferred to have a little wine with their lunch, but he had a pretty good feeling they wouldn't be staying the night — not yet, at least. And Tyler would never consider drinking and driving.

When they finished eating, he didn't fail to notice that Elena was looking at her watch. She was nervous being there alone with him. Good. She made him feel all sorts of inexplicable emotions. Throwing her off her game a little was justice in his book.

He stood up and said, "Let's go for a walk along the shore."

"We really should get back, Tyler. This has all been wonderful, but I have work to do"

"A small walk to help with digestion. And it's a Saturday. Work can wait."

Tyler had to smile after saying that. Though he wasn't quite the workaholic his brothers were, he didn't count weekends as work-free time zone. There were always things that could be done. Sometimes progress was easier when the phone wasn't ringing quite as much.

"A walk actually sounds pretty good," Elena told him.

They moved down a trail that took them to the water's edge, and then strolled along the small beach. The sun was shining, a nice breeze was blowing, and a few boats decorated the water with brilliant colors.

"I think this is where I would live if I had a choice," Elena told him with a happy sigh.

"It's too much of a commute," Tyler said, "and not nearly as nice in the winter."

She'd managed to walk too far away from him so far, so he closed the gap between them and took her hand. Surprisingly he enjoyed the feel of her fingers in his. He found himself rubbing the back of her hand with his thumb, loving her soft skin, and the way she shivered next to him.

"Yes, but I think it would be worth the long commute," she said.

"Why don't you live out this way then, or outside of the city?"

She paused in her steps, almost not noticeably, and then she began walking easily next to him, but he didn't miss the sudden tension in her.

"How do you know I don't? We don't know anything about each other. I could have a house on each of these islands for all you know," she said with a laugh.

"We might be a mystery to each other, but I'm good at reading people. You love it here, but it's clear from what you said that you don't have to commute so you obviously don't live on the islands. My guess is that you live pretty close to your work — walking distance, or at least a short bus ride."

She didn't look at him as they moved forward, and she took so long answering that he wondered if she was just going to ignore his comment.

"That's a pretty good guess. Too bad you won't find out. At least not today."

"Are you going to share anything about yourself?" Mystery was good. But this was getting a little ridiculous.

As if she could sense him pulling from her, she turned and smiled at him. "Well, you know about my best friend, Piper. She's the most important person in my life. I couldn't live without her. So that's knowing something."

"What about family?"

"I don't have any left."

"That's pretty sad. I can't imagine not having my brothers. We fight sometimes, but we're always there for each other."

"I was an only child and I lost my dad when I was very young. Check that. *Lost* isn't quite the word. He decided my mother and I weren't good enough for him. My mom died several years ago. So now it's Piper — only Piper."

She laughed as if this weren't a big deal, but he could hear the pain in her voice. She wasn't as good an actress as she seemed to think she was.

"Some people just weren't meant to procreate," Tyler told her. "Unfortunately, they sometimes do." It wasn't as if he were the person to give her any advice on parents. They didn't get worse than the ones he'd been given.

"I fully agree with you there! But here I am, for better or for worse."

They fell into silence and walked a while longer before he led her back to the cabin. He wanted to ask a thousand questions, but at the same time, he wanted to respect her privacy.

He was in uncharted territory with Elena.

They stepped back up to the cabin deck and he brought her inside, then slowly backed her up against the wall.

"I need to taste you again, Elena."

Before she even thought of uttering a protest, he leaned forward and captured her lips in a hungry kiss that showed her how much she affected him. She groaned into his mouth before winding her arms around him and giving back as much as she was getting.

His fingers dug into her hair as he turned her head, needing, wanting, hoping this was going to lead them straight into the master bedroom.

After he'd given her sweet lips a few more lingering caresses, those hands of hers, which had been gripping his shoulders, shifted and she ran them across his chest and then pushed.

Tyler leaned back only the slightest bit, in a daze. "What?" he asked, and his hoarse voice surprised him.

"It's time to get me home, Tyler. I really do need to work."

Her eyes were filled with passion, her body quivering in his embrace, but she was telling him no. Tyler felt it in his bones that he could change her mind. She wanted him, even if she felt she needed to wait. Maybe it was a three-date rule or something. *Women, women, women ...*

Tyler normally didn't date women who were so prudish. He liked sex, didn't like waiting, and didn't want to have to stick around when he didn't want to. He was breaking all sorts of rules with Elena.

And it seemed to be worth it.

CHAPTER NINE

"THIS WOMAN IS driving me insane!"

Tyler looked down at his phone for the hundredth time in a thirty-minute span.

"Well, then," Blake said, "she's obviously not the one for you if you're getting this riled up so soon after you've met."

"Here's the problem — I can't get her off my mind. We sent texts back and forth for a week before I finally got her to go to lunch with me. We had a nice time, took a walk, then had a kiss that has left me hard all week, and now I can't pin her down for another freaking date."

"Then maybe she's just messing with you," Blake said, "and you're better off to let this one go."

"I know that!" Tyler was beyond frustrated. Again he looked at his phone. Nothing. Zip. Zilch.

"So why are you storming around your office and acting like a bear?"

"Because I can't stop thinking about her," Tyler yelled.

"Okay. Then do something about it," Blake replied calmly.

"What? Kidnap the woman? I don't even know where she lives."

"Kidnapping might be a little extreme," Blake told him. "But I'm sure you have ways of finding out where she is. Find out whether she's playing games."

"Oh, believe me, I know she's playing games," Tyler said. "I just don't know what the prize is."

"Then you'd best figure it out."

"I have no effing idea what she could be after," Tyler said. "It's not as if she's going to get anything out of me."

"There are a lot of things a woman could get out of you," Blake told him.

"Only if I'm willing to give them."

Blake laughed. "It seems you'd be willing to give just about anything right now."

"Yeah, I know. And she has me so damn worked up, I'd just about sell my soul to take her to bed."

"Then she might just have you exactly where she wants you," Blake told him.

"That's the thing that pisses me off the most," Tyler snapped.

"Seriously, Tyler, you might want to let this one go."

"Don't look at me like that, Blake."

"Like what, Tyler?"

"Like I'm some pathetic sex-starved idiot."

"You're sure as hell acting like it."

"Well, I'm not. I'm doing just fine," Tyler insisted.

And then he froze when his phone buzzed. He would not look. He would not look. *He would not look!*

"Dammit!" He was practically shouting again as he lifted his phone up and looked.

Blake said nothing.

Tyler was close to having a mental breakdown, and he knew that he really should just delete this woman. She'd been trouble since the moment he'd approached her in the bar two weeks ago, and since then his world had been spinning off its axis. If he was this consumed with her before they even made it to bed, he'd most likely find himself in a hell of a lot more trouble once the deed was done.

Sorry I took so long to reply. I've been working.

"That's it. She takes two hours to get back to me, and she hardly says anything," Tyler muttered. Thankfully, Blake still remained silent.

Are we on for dinner at the Pink Door? Hey, Tyler could keep it short and to the point as well.

The clock ticked as he waited … and waited.

Dinner sounds great. I'll meet you there at 7.

I will pick you up at 6 and take you to the restaurant. He wanted to know where she lived, dammit. And he wanted her to tell him.

Sorry, but I'm coming straight from work. I'll just meet you there.

Should he argue? Nah. Tyler knew it wouldn't get him anywhere. This woman was more stubborn than he was — that was for sure. Maybe Blake was right. Maybe he really should just cancel.

He tossed his phone down and walked out of his office without both-ering to offer a word of explanation to his brother. What else could he say? At this point, he simply sounded like … a pouting baby. And that wasn't who he was.

Tyler left the Knight Construction offices and walked down to his favorite coffee stand. After grabbing a hot Americano, he made his way to the small park nearby and took a walk around one of the trails.

He'd left his phone behind, and that was something he never did. No one did that anymore. No one sane, anyway. But all week this woman had been playing him. She'd often send him a message — usually steamy — and like the sap he was, he'd reply, probably way too quickly, and then he wouldn't hear from her for hours, or sometimes even until the next day.

Tyler didn't play games. He'd told her that in the bar. Okay, so he'd said, "Let the games begin," but he hadn't meant it. Not really. Not in that sense. What made the entire situation so damn awful was that he was allowing her to game him this way. He knew what she was doing and yet he wasn't pulling back.

By the time he made his way back to his office, he decided he was done. That was it. He was going to cancel dinner. It was decided. After all, he was Tyler freaking Knight. If she wasn't going to respect him, then he wasn't about to waste his precious time on cheap trash like her. The world was full of women who wouldn't jerk him around, and who would make excellent bed companions.

He felt good in his decision. Even forced a halfway decent smile to pop up on his lips.

That was until he reached his office and picked up his phone. Once he saw the picture Elena had sent him while he was gone, his brain fried.

Dinner was most certainly back on … and dessert was essential.

CHAPTER TEN

TUCKED AWAY IN Pike Place Market, and definitely not an easy restaurant to find, the Pink Door was a classic Seattle destination, and Elena had wanted to check it out for quite some time.

That Tyler had chosen this location surprised her. She really hadn't taken him for a dinner-and-cabaret type of guy. She stepped from her cab and walked down the alley toward the restaurant.

Elena instantly spotted Tyler. He looked far too suave in his custom-tailored suit, which hugged his shoulders to perfection and cinched in at his waist to show how well-built he was. The man was tall, a few inches above six feet, and with his dark hair and blue eyes, and that come-and-get-me grin, he was doubtless a fantasy man come to life. For most women.

It was a good thing she wasn't most women.

She would have to tell herself this continuously if she spent much more time with the man. It hadn't been easy for her to keep stringing him along, to maintain this game of hers as long as she had, and she'd been doing it at a distance for days. Now, they were getting up close and personal again. She'd had to remind herself that he was a cold, ruthless businessman who didn't care how many people he ruined on his mission to become the best of the best.

47

Screw him! She squared her shoulders, and the small amount of guilt she'd been feeling fled. She decided she was going to go through with this. After all, men like Tyler never felt pain. Even if the pain she was able to inflict was minuscule, she hoped to do some damage to his monumental ego. Even a dent would be worth the effort. A chip off his blockhead.

All of the Knight brothers lived by their own rules and took whatever they wanted whenever they wanted it. Obviously. They took and took until there was nothing else to take and then they walked away without ever looking back. Like everyone in the worthless .01 percent.

Elena wasn't a fool. She didn't believe that anything she could do would make a huge impact on this insensitive man. But if she got just a hint of revenge, she could go to sleep knowing she'd done something for the lower classes. And we were all lower classes nowadays, or almost all of us. Us versus them.

He spun toward her when she was only a few feet away, and the power of his look made her stop in her tracks. Her stomach tightened as they engaged in a stare-off, and then he came forward, and he was within two inches of her. Whoa.

"I wasn't sure you would show up," he said, his voice a low rumble that made her body react in a way she absolutely didn't want it to do.

"I wasn't sure I would come." She couldn't stop those words.

"I like your honesty. Shall we?" He held out his arm, but she didn't move.

He raised an eyebrow in question, and she took a fortifying breath before placing her arm in his. Though she was expecting the electrical shock, it still sucked out her last remaining oxygen when it came. How was she going to carry through with her plan when she couldn't control her body's reaction to his?

"I have to do this."

Before she knew what he meant or what was happening, he backed her up against the brick wall and pressed his body against hers. And then his head descended and his lips were on hers. She told herself not to give in to him, but her body betrayed her yet again. Her hands reached up and gripped his arms and her lips fell open.

What started as a tingling in her body flared up into a supernova, and she forgot all about her plans of revenge, all about making this man sweat. *He* was the one making *her* sweat, making her forget where she was — who she was.

"That was just a taste of what it will be like between us," Tyler said.

It took a moment for her to realize that he'd stopped kissing her, that he'd now back. She opened her eyes and tried to focus on his face. When she did, her temper quickly quenched the fire that had been burning inside her.

His smug expression told her more about the man than any of his smarmy words could. He knew he was gorgeous, knew he was a fantastic lover, knew he could get or have anything he wanted. Well, this poor little rich boy wouldn't have her — at least not again. But he sure as hell would want to.

She said nothing as she turned toward the famous pink door and opened it herself. She wasn't giving him the satisfaction of letting him act like the gentleman he was *pretending* to be. They stepped inside, the ambience of the restaurant warm and inviting, with candles offering soft lighting and the tables set in a charming way.

They were escorted to an elevated table with an excellent view of the stage, and soon their waiter brought them appetizers and drinks. The food placed before them — oysters, pasta, breads and cheeses — was too much for anyone to consume, unless you were a football player or an underpaid newspaper reporter. Of course when you never went without, the thought of wasting food didn't even cross your mind. And she was sure that it wasn't crossing his.

When the jazz band began to play and its soft music drifted around them, Elena knew why Tyler had chosen this restaurant. The entire scene was nothing more than foreplay, a place to prepare a date for a romantic night with sex on the menu at the end. Romantic? She was old-fashioned enough to think that romance wasn't quite so calculating or so cold.

He was good, very good. Smooth. But he couldn't fool her so easily — she wouldn't let him entrap her with all the moves she was sure he'd used a thousand times before.

"I can't figure you out, Elena. One moment you laugh with me, flirt with me, open up, even. The next, you're ducking your head, apparently thinking up a storm but showing nothing of what those thoughts are. What are you up to?"

Tyler picked up his wineglass and took a sip. She shifted in her seat. If he was this observant already, she would never be able to pull this off. She took a drink of her own wine before carefully choosing her response.

"I don't date a whole lot," she said. "To tell you the truth, it scares me a bit. I'm sorry if it appears that I'm not interested." She hoped that her reply would throw him off the scent.

"I have no doubt that you're interested," he told her, making her want to smack him. "I can just see that you aren't too happy about feeling that way."

"What makes you think that you know me so well after we've seen each other only a few times?"

"I don't know what it is about you, but there's something familiar. Have we met before?"

That hit a way too close to home. She didn't want him to know they'd been childhood friends, and she really didn't want him to know about the men's club. Not yet, she didn't, maybe not ever. It was too humiliating.

"No. I would certainly remember meeting you, Tyler," she told him with what she hoped was a saucy laugh.

"Still, I don't know ..." As he trailed off, he finally broke their eye contact.

Good. She didn't want to talk much. She just wanted to get this night over with. Maybe she should speed up her plan. He had seduction on the brain, so wouldn't now be the perfect opportunity?

No. She wasn't strong enough yet to carry through. And she didn't think he was hooked on her enough. She had to make an impact when she walked out on him.

Before she could make a decision one way or the other, Tyler stood up and held out a hand.

"Let's dance."

The way he said the words, he might as well have been telling her to drop her pants and let him take her right there. Seduction was burned into every fiber of Tyler's being.

"If I recall correctly, this isn't the first time you've asked me to dance."

"But this time we'll do that dance, Elena."

She suddenly found herself pulled from her chair and being led to the intimate dance area.

Tyler didn't pause as he pulled her close, making her feel like it was only the two of them on the floor the moment his arms wound behind her back. The instant sizzle between the two of them should have frightened her enough to pull away, but instead she found her hands drifting upward until they rested on the back of his neck.

"Do you come here often, Tyler?" She was only speaking to break the intensity of the moment. His next words didn't help with that.

"While dancing, there should never be talking. It's a prelude to things to come," he whispered, his breath fanning against her ear as he pulled her a little bit closer.

"It's just a dance," she said, infusing laughter she didn't feel into her voice.

"Pay close attention, Elena. You'll soon see that it's never just a dance."

Then his arms tightened behind her back, one shifting lower as he pressed her forward, allowing her to feel his hardness against her midsection. He tucked her head against him as he leaned down and ran his lips against the edge of her ear, his hot breath sending a shudder rippling through her.

His scent, his breath, his bulging muscles all surrounded her, pressed into her, entrapped her in a moment when the rest of the world fell away and it was just the two of them.

Elena had to pull away now. But her effort misfired. When she drew back, she was then looking right into Tyler's eyes, and what was reflected back at her took her breath away.

Passion. Excitement. Hunger. So much hunger.

She didn't know who moved first, but suddenly their lips were clasped together and she felt like a person lost in the desert getting her first sip of water in days.

Her fingers tightened behind his neck as she greedily sipped from his lips, submerging herself in the passion that flowed so easily and so powerfully between them. For a brief instant Elena forgot that he was the enemy, forgot that she had an agenda. She forgot everything except for the way he was making her feel.

When he broke away, she whimpered, and the passion in his gaze leapt even higher.

"Let me take you home," he said, his voice pure silk.

It took a moment for the words to make their mark inside Elena's muddled brain, but when they did, she immediately tensed. There was no way she was ready for this, not yet, not after that scorching kiss.

"I … um … not tonight," she said, and then pulled from him. She was almost surprised when he released her. But she didn't understand her disappointment when he did it.

They walked back to the table, and Elena couldn't make herself sit back down. She couldn't continue this night any longer. She was feeling too weak. It was probably temporary. All she had to do was rebuild the walls around her heart, she convinced herself. No problem.

"It's been a wonderful night, Tyler, but I'm beginning to get a headache. I think it best if I go home a little early."

His eyes narrowed just a little, but he recovered. Turning from her without saying a word, he signaled for the waiter. And then he escorted her out of the restaurant. The cool night air felt good, so good. She would regroup, figure out her next move, and get this entire plan of hers — this plan, which didn't seem quite so great anymore — out of the way.

"I'll take you home," he said, and it wasn't a question.

"I can get home just fine," she said right back.

"I always make sure my dates get home safely, Elena. I take you home or this thing between us is done."

His words weren't harsh, just matter-of-fact. She wanted to walk away, to tell him to go to hell. But she knew that if she did that, she'd never have her victory.

"Fine. You can take me home," she said in a taut voice.

He walked her to his car and held open the door. She gave him her address, then sat back, fuming. This wasn't going well — not well at all. And she'd thought she was so smart. Maybe she'd forgotten that revenge was a dish best served cold, and she was still too hot. Too hot with everything to do about Tyler Knight.

She knew she had to do something to salvage this situation, but how?

They pulled up to her apartment complex, hardly the best place in the city, but far from the worst. He parked and came around to the passenger side.

She allowed him to open her door and help her from the low-slung sports car. And then the two of them walked to her door.

She wheeled around before she inserted her key into the lock, and she smiled at him. "Thank you for dinner. The place was even better than I'd expected. I've wanted to go there for quite some time."

"Thank you for accompanying me, Elena. I had a wonderful evening."

"Really?"

"Didn't you enjoy yourself?" he asked, taking a step closer to her.

"Yes, but then, you know, the headache," she said with a nervous giggle. Oh, no. A *giggle*. What had she become?

"Do I make you uncomfortable, Elena?" he asked before lifting a hand and running his fingers through her hair.

"No ... no." Was she stuttering? What an utter disaster. Just kill her now and get it over with. Stick a fork into her. Hmm. *Fork* or ...

"I think I do. I think that it scares the hell out of you." He moved the last few inches forward.

"I think you're awfully full of yourself," she told him.

He leaned down and spoke against the corner of her mouth. "I am *very* sure of myself."

She could push him away, tell him the night was over, but that wasn't what a seductress would do. No, a woman who wanted a man to pant over her the rest of the night would grab him, initiate the kiss.

So that's exactly what she did.

She took control of his mouth, kissing him with everything she had.

Soon, the kiss had her knees shaking, had her body on fire, and still she carried on. She was running her hands up the back of his head and pulling him even closer. This was so much more intimate than in the restaurant because she knew a nice comfortable bed was only a door — well, two doors — away. Precision was always important in her line of work.

She couldn't think things like that about her bed! It was a game … She was forgetting that, though, the longer his lips caressed hers.

His fingers glided up and down her side before he cupped her bottom and pulled her up. He was so hard. The ache flaming inside her neglected body reminded her that it had been way too long since she'd felt something like satisfaction with a man — with this man.

The longer he touched her, the more she was reminded of that night in the limo. It had been amazing — that was, until he'd dismissed her so coolly and so callously.

This situation wasn't good at all!

When he pulled back, his eyes dilated, his breathing heavy, she wondered whether she would be able to stop when the time came. What if they both came? That would ruin her plan.

"Good night, Elena."

Tyler shocked her when he turned her key in her door, pushed her inside, shut the door, and then walked away. She didn't move for at least two minutes. Her breathing took that long to get under control.

If each meeting with Tyler left her this off balance, she really should abort her mission. Then again, Elena had never been a quitter.

CHAPTER ELEVEN

"**D**O YOU WANT some company?"

Elena choked on the bite of sandwich she'd just taken when Tyler made his sudden appearance. He quickly began patting her back, and she finally managed to swallow and then reached for her drink.

"What are you doing here, Tyler?"

"I was in the area and saw you sitting here," he said. He joined her on the bench once he was assured he wasn't going to have to give her the Heimlich maneuver.

"You were in the park, this park, on a Tuesday afternoon?"

Tyler smiled as he watched her trying to process why he was there. He wasn't one to leave things in the air. It hadn't taken him long to figure out Elena's last name, and from there to figure out where she worked — and where she enjoyed eating her lunch.

They'd been seeing each other for three weeks now, and he had no doubt that she was messing with him. They'd been on only a few outings. Most of their interactions had been over the phone, and she still shared nothing about herself with him. He knew he should cut his losses and walk away, but he couldn't.

"Yes, I come here often," he said. "It's a great place to run, or to come to sit down for lunch. Sometimes I enjoy simply sitting on the benches and letting my mind clear of all the chaos from a busy day."

"I … um … just didn't realize you worked around here," she finally muttered.

"We've never talked about my work, so how would you know where I spend my days?"

He could see he had her flustered. He'd been pretty sure she had known exactly who he was from the first time they'd met in the bar. Now, he had no doubts. This woman was after something; was it some sort of extortion? He didn't see how she could possibly pull that off. Maybe that was why he was still seeing her. Because he hated to have questions go unanswered.

"I guess that makes sense," she said, quickly recovering with a forced laugh. Then she placed her hand on his leg and gently rubbed it.

Her ploy of touching him so he would quit asking questions almost worked. After all, he wanted this woman so badly that he was pretty much walking around with a permanent erection. But it was Tyler's turn to be in control. Though her touch sent flames through his body, he also knew that his touch on her caused her intelligence to dim. So he fought back by grabbing her hand and winding his fingers through hers.

The problem with all the physical contact was that he wasn't sure who it affected more, him or her. Only time was going to tell. He would have this woman, though — that was something he had no doubt about.

"You must work nearby," he said, looking out toward a group of office buildings.

"Yes, not far from here. If it's a nice day, and it isn't very often here, I enjoy coming down to the park for lunch and a walk. I was just getting ready for a little exercise," she said, pulling her hand away from his and gathering up what was left of her takeout meal.

She got up and threw the leftovers and the wrappings in a nearby trash bin.

"I have time," he told her. "I'll walk with you. Then you can show me where you work." And he linked their hands together again.

"If I take you by my workplace, we won't have any mystery between us anymore. Things won't be nearly as exciting," she said, again with the shaky laugh.

"At what point do we just open up?" he said, stopping her when they came to a stand of trees.

He walked her a little off the trail so they could have some privacy.

"What's the rush, Tyler? We're having a good time," she said, resisting him, but only a little.

"I'm not in a hurry, Elena. I just might want to know a little bit more about the woman I plan on taking to my bed."

"Do you always know the women you take to your bed?"

Tyler was taken aback by the hostility of that question.

"Since I've grown up, I do," he said with hesitation.

"So not always." It wasn't a question.

"No, not always. You know what they say about boys being boys," he told her with a laugh he didn't feel.

Her eyes narrowed the slightest bit before she masked her expression. "Yeah, I guess boys will be boys," she told him. "Great excuse for bad behavior. It's a wonder that men are allowed to be president — they're just too emotional, too unreliable. Is it okay by you if girls will be girls?"

"What is going on here, Elena?"

"Nothing. I've just got a lot on my mind and I wasn't expecting to see you down here today. That's all," she said, and she brushed up against him.

Tyler had already figured out that when she wanted him to stop talking, she initiated physical contact. Who was he to push her away? It's all he wanted from her, right?

That thought didn't sit too well with him — not in his new way of thinking — but he had to harden himself. She was obviously after money. It was the only thing he could think of. She was a lawyer, but she'd only been practicing for a couple of years, and he was sure she'd built up quite a bit of debt going to school, and living in Seattle. Her apartment was nice, but she had a roommate. Still, a two-bedroom in a decent area of Seattle wasn't cheap.

What Tyler couldn't figure out was how she was planning on exploiting him. And why he was allowing this to continue? Did he want her that badly?

Apparently he did.

"What do you want from me, I wonder," Tyler said, trailing his fingers down her cheek.

"Why don't you stop wondering and give me a kiss before I have to get back to work?" she said.

She wound her hands behind his head and pulled him to her. It didn't matter how many times their mouths touched. His body exploded with each brush of their lips.

He'd never actually put this much effort into being with a woman before. Yes, he'd had a few longer-term relationships, including the one with the woman he'd been about to propose to, but those had started so much simpler, and he'd definitely bedded all of the others a lot faster than this. *Three freaking weeks without lift-off?* For that matter, without "freaking" …

"I want you, Elena," he growled, breaking away from those tempting lips. "Tonight."

She shook her head slightly, obviously trying to clear her thoughts. He could see that she was as turned on as he was. Why was she continuing to stall? Maybe she was just a tease.

"Patience, Tyler. The longer we wait, the better it will be."

"I've waited plenty long enough, Elena."

"Then I guess a little while longer won't kill you," she said, taking one step back, and then several steps more.

"This conversation isn't finished yet," he told her. Reaching down, he untucked his shirt trying to cover up the effect she had on him. From the way he was throbbing, scraping painfully against his jeans, he doubted he'd manage to be presentable in public anytime soon.

The saucy little minx obviously knew it, too.

"Gotta go. See you later."

And she turned and practically ran away.

Tyler leaned against the tree and took deep, steadying breaths. What he should do was march into her office, bend her over, and take her right there on her desk.

No, not his style. He would wait. But not much longer.

CHAPTER TWELVE

ELENA FOUND HERSELF smiling even as she walked down a claustrophobic Seattle sidewalk. So many people. So she really didn't understand her smile; she just knew that she was in a good mood. The only negative was the fact that she'd spent a lot of time with Tyler this past month, and she was getting used to it, getting fond of his phone calls and of having him around.

After his sneak attack in the park last week, she'd had no choice but to let her guard down slightly. He'd been growing far too suspicious, and her plan would never work if he was constantly analyzing everything she did. So a couple days later, when he'd asked her to go to dinner, she hadn't hesitated.

The problem had been the walk through the park after dinner. She was getting far too comfortable with the man, and he was making her laugh much too easily without even trying much.

Could she go on with this? She sincerely hoped so. Or maybe she didn't.

She stopped and stared at the door before her in surprise, and then she double-checked her phone to make sure this was where she was supposed to be.

This wasn't the sort of place where a billionaire like Tyler would hang out. But it was the address that he'd given her. And the name stenciled on the front window confirmed it: *Nascosto*. It seemed to be a bit of a dive, and she was happy at the thought. Was he human after all?

Once she walked through the doorway, she glanced around and found Tyler sitting by the bar with one of his brothers. They both looked a little grim. She hadn't wanted to run into any of his brothers. Tyler was her only target. The more involved she became in this, the harder it was going to be when the walls came crashing down. Scorn one brother and maybe they wouldn't care so much, but scorn them all, and certainly they would seek some revenge of their own. *Think about it*, she told herself. *Billionaires are dangerous. They didn't become so rich by playing nice.*

But she wasn't about to wimp out at the first hurdle. Screw these fat cats. So, pasting a smile on her face, she walked up with an air of what she hoped to be total confidence and draped her arm around Tyler. Let his brother think what he wanted.

"I'm sorry I'm so late," she said with a rueful glance.

"It's not a problem," Tyler replied. "I was talking to my brother here."

"Oh, your brother!" she exclaimed, and then almost winced at her faux enthusiasm. She should have studied acting in college. "It's a pleasure to meet you."

Then Elena shocked herself when she stepped forward and gave the guy a hug. What in the world was she thinking? Her nerves had taken charge and screwed her over.

"What ever happened to handshakes?" remarked Byron, one of Tyler's brothers.

She was instantly filled with hurt, and she didn't know why. She'd barely spent any time with either Byron or Blake when she'd been young, but still, it stung that he too had zero recollection of her. Hadn't she made an impression on any of these men? Clearly not. He was just another of the wealthy elite who wouldn't notice, let alone socialize with, little ol' her.

She kept her smile firmly in place — she wasn't about to let him know that his careless comment had affected her in the least — and she looked him directly in the eyes.

"Sorry," she told Byron. "I'm impulsive."

"We'll leave you to brood, big brother," Tyler said. He stood up and wrapped his arm around Elena, and he led her away.

When they got outside, Elena wanted to shake his arm off, still feeling the sting of Byron's rejection, but she somehow managed to keep from showing how much the man had hurt her. Another Knight with less than shining armor.

"I thought we were eating there," she said when they walked farther down the street.

"I was going to, but with my brother in a bear of a mood, I thought it would be safer to try somewhere else," he said. He ushered her into a parking garage.

"Where are we going?" This wasn't in her plans.

"I'm going to surprise you," he told her, and he flipped her a wink before walking up to his car and holding the passenger door open.

"I have things I need to do this afternoon," she said. And she didn't step in.

"I won't keep you out too late, Elena … unless you want to."

"Fine." She climbed in and waited for him to come around to the driver's side.

He revved up his fancy little car, and then they were heading away from the city. The farther they got away, the more nervous Elena became. When they turned off the freeway and began entering what appeared to be a gated community — hell, it was more than gated; it was exclusive in the extreme, not for plebeians like her — her stomach dropped.

"I want to show you my actual home, not just my cabin," he said as he pulled up, entered a code, and then began driving down a long and fancy paved road. No. It wasn't a gated community. Silly of her even to think that. It was an estate, his estate.

"I guess this is a surprise," she told him quietly. She was nervous. Incredibly nervous.

"There's nothing to worry about. I just thought it would be nice to show you where I live. I have a great view of the water," he said. And he pulled into a massive garage attached to a house that would make the word *mansion* sound pitiful. What was wrong with this guy?

"I'm sure you have the best view. Isn't that your style?" She couldn't help herself. She'd said that with just a bit of scorn.

He looked at her questioningly, but he didn't comment.

She knew she needed to tone it back a little. She was now used to having him open car doors, so she waited until he came around to her side, then she took his hand as he helped her out.

They stepped into a hallway that led to an enormous kitchen. A kitchen with the dream equipment of every chef in the world, professional or wannabe.

"Do you cook more than just steaks on a grill?" she asked, a little in awe. He was apparently more accomplished in the kitchen than she'd imagined of such an overprivileged guy.

"I'm actually a fantastic cook, which is why I decided to bring you here. How do lobster rolls and chowder sound?"

Her stomach rumbled at the words. "Fantastic."

"Do you want the tour first, or are you more interested in a little food?"

"I don't need a tour right now," she told him. She was somehow able to pull away and walk over to the adjoining dining room, where large windows showed off the excellent view he'd been boasting about. "Impressive," she had to confess.

"It's why I bought the property. I love the water. Go on it every chance I get. Maybe after lunch I can talk you into a boat ride."

"It's a bit chilly today," she said. She would have loved to take that boat ride, but she had to remind herself that she wasn't really dating this man. It was all for payback. Payback … Why had the idea of exacting revenge somehow lost a lot of its appeal? Was she going soft?

"Seattle weather turns on a dime. Let's have a little bit to eat and see how it feels afterward. Let me make you a drink, and you can either come into the kitchen and watch me work, or you can enjoy the deck."

He made her an iced mint green tea with an alcoholic twist, which was both refreshing and had just the right amount of a kick to it to help her nerves. She wanted so much to sit in the kitchen and watch him. But she wanted it far too much, so she decided to wander out to the deck, if only to save her sanity.

The cool breeze had her quickly coming back inside, though. Nope. No boating any time in the near future.

Sitting down at the large kitchen island, she watched as Tyler played the part of a "Chopped" chef.

"Do you want to eat here or over in the dining room?"

"Here's fine. I like this island. I don't think I've ever seen one quite so large."

"I like big things; I've got a lot of them," he said as he set a plate and bowl before her.

Elena was praying that what he'd whipped up wouldn't be delicious, because Tyler didn't need anything more about him to make him *seem* even more perfect. But her first bite into the lobster roll ruined that hope. Yummmm.

"Okay, I don't want to admit it, but you do know how to cook," she told him as she wiped the corner of her mouth delicately with a linen napkin.

"I get tired of going out, so about ten years ago, I bought a dozen cookbooks and took some classes to help teach me. I caught on fast. Some people like to do it; some don't. I find cooking enjoyable. Calming, in fact."

"Most men wouldn't admit to that Tyler."

"Hey! The best cooks out there are men," he told her with a wink. "Like Gordon Ramsay."

"Of course. A sad fellow with an ego problem who shouts at everyone and doesn't even wear underwear. That got the poor guy burned. But point proven," she shot back, a real smile slipping past her.

"Ah, but when people taste his masterpieces, they don't care about his attitude."

"I care. I refuse to buy anything that man has his name on."

"You hold quite a grudge against people who you don't find worthy, don't you?" he said with that analytical look in his eyes again.

Elena panicked. If he figured this out before she carried through on her plans, she would be left the victim once again. No, no, no. That couldn't happen.

"Even the noblest of people can hold a grudge," she said with a laugh, "at least on a bad day. But I consider myself pretty mellow."

"I don't know if I can agree with that. I'll need a little more time to figure you out, Elena. Not that I'll consider any of it wasted."

They finished dinner and Elena excused herself. She stood in front of the bathroom mirror for quite some time while she tried to talk herself out of going through with her plan.

But as she looked at her reflection, the woman gazing back at her wasn't the same young kid she'd once been. Tyler had stolen something from her in her youth, and then he'd slapped her back down again when she was at another vulnerable stage in her life. It wasn't right. He deserved to suffer.

Squaring her shoulders, then undoing a couple of buttons on her blouse, Elena decided it was now or never.

"Let the games begin," she whispered, despite the sadness that was filling her.

Then she went to find Tyler.

CHAPTER THIRTEEN

W HEN ELENA RETURNED to the kitchen, her nosebleed heels clicked on the tile floor as she sauntered toward him. Damn, Tyler loved the way her legs looked in those sexy shoes, and he loved how her hips were swinging as she moved closer. How could he help but pant like a pathetic dog as she glided slowly and inexorably toward him?

He couldn't miss that some buttons were now undone on her top, and his gaze fastened on the bit of cleavage on display that hadn't been visible earlier. Something was happening here, but what it was wasn't exactly clear. He saw a new purpose in Elena's eyes, a major change since he'd picked her up a few hours ago.

He stood there as she came closer and closer and closer. His heart was racing but he knew it didn't show in his face. He wouldn't give her that easy victory, not after all the work she'd put him through over the past month.

But dammit if he didn't want her in his bed right this minute. He wanted her clothes stripped away. He wanted to have her writhing and screaming beneath him. He wanted her fingers on him, and he wanted it to continue the rest of the day and all night.

"Thanks for dinner," she said in a low purr as she lifted a hand and trailed her fingers down his arm.

"My pleasure," he said. He fought to keep his cool, but he couldn't. He snaked out an arm and wrapped it around her. "What are you doing, Elena?"

"I'm still hungry," she said, her warm breath blowing against his neck as she leaned in and kissed the skin right over his pounding pulse.

That kiss made his already hard body pulse with the need to sheath itself in her heat.

He curved his hands over her succulent behind, and then leaned down, brushing his lips against hers as he spoke.

"I can handle that hunger of yours, Elena. All you have to do is say the word." He kissed her lips now, but with only a bit more intensity. He knew something about subtlety.

The low moan that traveled up through her throat made him lose his cool. Way too fast. He was trying to keep in control here, but how could he do it? She was pressed up against him, and only a few layers of fabric separated his skin from hers. He wasn't feeling subtle now. But he was sure feeling her.

"You say you can handle it, but you aren't doing much to do that." After leveling that taunt at him, she pushed her hips forward and rubbed against his hardness.

With a speed born of incredible lust, Tyler undid the button of her tan capri slacks and lowered them so quickly it made her eyes widen. She didn't say a word as he lifted her body so the slacks floated to the floor, and then he kicked them away.

Without an ounce of hesitation, he set her down and pulled her against him, returning his hands to her nearly naked behind. The panties she wore were hardly a barrier between him and what he wanted.

"Still hungry, Elena?"

She was panting as she looked at him in shock. "Yes," she finally moaned as he squeezed her firm buttocks.

Leaning in, she pressed hot kisses to his neck as he undid the rest of the buttons on her blouse and parted it. The soft blue material served as a nice frame to her body as she stood before him with only the lace of her bra and her panties now keeping him from seeing what he wanted to see most.

She pulled his shirt free from his trousers, then her hands snuck upward and she ran her fingernails along the taught skin of his stomach and chest. She squeezed his nipples lightly, sending a bolt of sensation all through him.

Enough of this! With one hand he gripped her head and tilted it. He ravished her mouth, giving her a taste of what he had planned for them in the next hour — hours — hell, days.

He released her only long enough to rip off his shirt, then grabbed her again, spinning her around and lifting her, setting her on the island, which just so happened to be the perfect height for him to grind his hardness against her very wet and barely covered core.

"Damn, you're responsive," he gasped He took a step back and gloried in the passionate flush covering her body.

"Hmm … I bet you say that to all the women you bring home."

"I don't bring women home," he told her.

By the look in her hooded eyes, he could see that she didn't believe him. Give her time and she would. Tyler wasn't some innocent schoolboy, but his house was sacred to him. He didn't like to bring women home, didn't like them invading his personal space. Not after his last relationship. All he wanted was peace when he walked through his front door. He hadn't planned on bringing Elena here, but somehow he'd found himself driving in this direction. And with her on perfect display on his kitchen island, he couldn't regret that decision.

"Lie back," he commanded her.

"What? Why?" Elena's eyes were darting around uneasily.

Instead of giving her any answer, he pushed her back against the smooth granite and then dropped to his knees and feasted on the sight of her silk-covered core.

Her protests died as he began trailing his fingers against the material, which was wet with her arousal. Then he slipped his finger underneath the thin elastic and without hesitation he pushed a finger inside her tight heat. She gasped, and her legs shook against the edge of the island.

Lifting those lovely legs, he put them on his shoulders as he leaned forward and ran his tongue up the silk of her panties.

"Tyler … no … we … shouldn't …." She stopped speaking when he shifted her panties aside and encircled her womanhood with his lips while he flicked his tongue over her swollen bud. She was now a quivering mass.

"You taste so good," he said before swiping his tongue over her slick folds and feasting on her bud again.

"Tyler!" Elena called out his name over and over again as he sucked and licked her into complete submission.

As he felt her body convulse, felt her nearing the release he desperately wanted to give her, he slipped a second finger inside her and began pumping. Suddenly she screamed and writhed on the counter before him, shudders running all through her as he drew out the pleasure for as long as she could handle it.

Only when she went completely limp beneath his touch did he pull his fingers from her and move upward to kiss her belly. It was still shaking.

He made his way upward, then kissed the skin exposed between her breasts as her chest heaved. He needed to taste her nipples — oh, how he needed that. So he unhooked the front clasp of her lacy little bra and peeled it away.

He ran his tongue over one peaked nipple and then the other until he had her crying out again. He pulled her back into a sitting position and pressed in closely to her, loving the way she felt in his arms. It caused him more agony, but he pressed his manhood against her soaked panties, letting her feel what her pleasure was doing to him.

He then cupped one breast and squeezed while he ran his lips along her neck, swirling his tongue against her flesh before gently nipping it. She jerked against him and moaned while she grasped his hair.

When he moved up and captured her lips again, he felt himself smile. Damn, he was falling hard for this woman — so hard. Would he ever be able to climb out from under her spell?

Tyler didn't think he wanted to.

"I want you in my bed," he said. He lifted her off the kitchen island and walked swiftly through his house to the large master bedroom.

After laying her down on top of the covers, he immediately pulled her against him, damning the trousers that he'd forgotten to take off.

"I don't think I've ever wanted someone as much as I've wanted you," he told her. Full disclosure. He wasn't afraid to hide what he was feeling right then and there.

She stiffened in his arms, and he saw her eyes grow wide.

"Oh, I have to … um … use … I have to … go to the bathroom," she told him.

Tyler moaned in frustration as she wriggled out of his grasp and practically ran away.

It was okay. When she came back he'd be more than ready for her.

With speed born out of desperation to sink inside her, he stripped off his remaining clothes and lay there on the bed, waiting. And wanting.

When she returned, he wasn't going to let her leave his bed again, not for at least twelve hours straight.

CHAPTER FOURTEEN

H E WAS PROBABLY wondering what she was doing there in his bathroom. Elena knew she'd been hiding out way too long, but it was taking her forever to stiffen her resolve.

She scrunched her eyes in the mirror and gave herself a stern look. "You knew this wasn't going to be easy, but if it teaches him even the smallest of lessons, you have accomplished what you set out to do. Just do it!"

Her pep talk to herself wasn't motivating her, unfortunately, so she washed her face with cool water and tried again. She was still overheated, still desperate for satisfaction despite all he'd given her there in the kitchen. All that heat on the cool granite.

She wanted more.

Maybe this "project" of hers was going to end up punishing her far more than it did him.

Too bad. No pain, no gain.

She finally stepped from the bathroom and leaned in the doorway, her shirt still unbuttoned but concealing a little more now, open just enough to show Tyler the curves of her breasts but not her still-hard nipples. Her panties were back in place, but she couldn't hide the flush on her cheeks, and as she looked at Tyler lying in the bed — buck naked — she was heating up all over again.

"Come back to my bed," he said, reaching out for her.

Elena looked down, then met his eyes and smiled. "Do you want me, Tyler?" she asked, moving a little closer.

"You know I do, baby," he said with a giant smile, while showing her just how much he wanted her. He was standing tall. And thick. And waiting.

"Good. Are you hurting?" She gave him her most seductive smile.

"Oh, yeah, baby. I'm hurting," he said. His tongue came out and wet his lips.

"Good. Then you're exactly where I want you to be."

He froze, his smile slowly fading at the sudden change in her tone. Her friskiness had vanished, and in its place was pure loathing, loathing directed right at him.

Tyler's jaw dropped. "What in the … hell is going on?"

"Are you confused?" she asked.

"Yeah, just a little," he told her. He sat up and pulled the blanket back over himself.

That was too bad. She'd been enjoying the view. Okay, maybe it was for the good. The view had been a little too enticing and messing with her head.

"You see, Tyler, I know exactly who you are. You're a spoiled, self-righteous little rich boy who thinks he can have anything he wants. Now that I've gotten you all worked up, you can think about the fact that sometimes even *you* won't get everything handed to you on a silver platter. Oh, wait. Maybe you billionaires deal in platinum platters."

Turning around, Elena smiled in victory. When she'd vowed to take Tyler Knight down, she hadn't realized how easy it would be to seduce him. Men like him should pay, though they rarely did.

She walked back into the bathroom and almost had the door shut when it was thrust back open. Standing there, looking far from pleased, was Tyler in all his naked glory.

"Don't think for even one second that you can make a comment like that and then just walk away," he said, and he took a menacing step toward her.

Elena's heart lodged in her throat. This game had just taken a direction she hadn't been planning on.

She'd expected slight anger, and frustration, of course. She hadn't expected the predatory look that she now saw in his eyes.

"I can do whatever I want to do, Tyler." Elena latched the front of her bra and then began doing up the buttons of her shirt. And he stood there looking at her as if she had two heads.

Maybe she did.

"What in the hell is your deal? For the past month you've been playing with me, and now this?" he thundered. "I knew something was up, but didn't expect such a sucker punch. You weren't looking at me with disgust in your eyes while I was devouring you on the kitchen island."

As he said this, he took a step closer, and Elena's heart pounded. She had to go on the offensive, and fast.

"You have no clue who I am, do you?" she snapped, poking him hard in the chest.

That question seemed to take him aback for a moment. He traced her face with his eyes, but no comprehension set in.

"Dammit, Elena, if I had slept with you before, I'd remember," he said. "I've had more than a few relationships — I'll admit that — but I don't forget the women I take to bed. What in the hell have I done to piss you off so badly?"

He wasn't letting her get around him in the bathroom, but thankfully, he wasn't touching her, either. She couldn't handle that right now. His statement crushed her more than she could have imagined it would.

No, he hadn't slept with her. He'd screwed her. And then tossed her aside and forgotten all about her.

"You Knights just take and take, and when you're finished doing that, you leave a wake behind you a mile long without once ever looking back. So, this might not have been the best plan in the world, but I wanted to make you feel something like loss — at least once in your life. You're selfish and hurtful and you deserve to want something that you can't have." Elena pushed against him, trying to get past.

Tyler grabbed both her wrists with one hand and held them above her head as he thrust her against the wall.

"Explain now."

His voice was now deadly calm, which was far worse than if he were yelling.

Her voice trembled slightly, but she spoke in a rush. "We knew each other once, Tyler, but I don't expect you to have any comprehension of that ..."

"When did I know you?" She could see the wheels spinning but nothing was hitting home.

"It doesn't matter, but there was a time I cared about you, and you so quickly and easily forgot about me. And then we saw each other again you might as well have thrown me to the wolves. Wait! That's exactly what you did. The person I once knew — I had thought was kind and he was my whole world. And then I watched you through the years, seeing all your exploits in the papers. You don't care about anyone but yourself. That's how your family operates. You're just like your father. He must have taught you well!"

Thunder was raging in Tyler's eyes as she continued speaking, but they narrowed dangerously when she brought up his dad. That might not have been the best move on her part, but none of her moves tonight had been that smooth. Anger had made her lash out. Fear made her say foolish things. And right now she was feeling both of those emotions.

"First of all, you will tell me how we know each other. If I've somehow wronged you, I deserve to know how," he said, the anger in his voice barely contained. He paused for a moment. "And I am nothing like the evil bastard who gave me life. I won't tolerate being compared to that man."

She should stop. She knew she should stop, but so many emotions were rushing through her and she couldn't seem to keep her damn mouth shut.

"Really? I disagree. I've studied you for years." She started choking on her words, and stopped before reminding him of their onetime friendship. He didn't know who she was and there was no reason to bring that up.

"I want to know who you are right now." He was so commanding, she almost told him. But somehow she stopped herself.

"It doesn't matter, Tyler. I don't want to be here. I don't want to be with you," she told him.

"I know more about you than you think."

"You don't know anything," she said, far less calmly than he had.

"Want to test it?"

"I want you to unhand me, unless you make a habit of forcing yourself on women," she said.

Tyler instantly released her and took a step back.

"Believe me, I don't need to force myself on anyone," he said before moving to the bathroom door and holding it wide open. "You can get the hell out of my house."

The coldness of his voice sent a shudder down her spine. Elena didn't say anything further; she just skirted around him and ran to his kitchen to find her slacks and shoes.

She grabbed them, put them on quickly, and left through his front door, shivers racking her body.

Now what was she supposed to do? He'd driven her there, and she had no idea where she was. She trudged despairingly to the end of his driveway, and that took her a good ten minutes. But when she reached the gate, a cab sat there waiting. *Phew!*

Still, it looked as if Tyler had sent more than one woman from his house this way if he could get a cab there that fast. She scrambled inside, gave the man her address, and used every power within her to keep herself from crying.

She'd been downgraded, not to mention degraded. Last time he'd screwed her, he'd at least offered her a limo ride home. Now, she was delegated to a stinky cab. It was her choice this time, though.

She'd done what she'd set out to do. It was just too damn bad that she felt like crap about it. Revenge had seemed so satisfying when she'd thought it up initially. Now, it just left her feeling hollow and more alone than she'd ever felt before.

CHAPTER FIFTEEN

"WHO IN THE hell does she think she is?"

Tyler's two brothers looked on in fascination. They'd been nearly silent for the past half an hour as he ranted on and on about Elena and her scheme. He couldn't stop himself.

Finally, he turned and actually looked at them. The two men were sitting in his library with their legs propped up, drinks in their hands, and ridiculously silly grins on their faces. Whatever happened to brotherly solidarity?

"Are you going to just sit there all night long or are you going to give me some input?" he snapped. He glared at them murderously.

"Well, considering you haven't given us two seconds to give any *input*, we thought we'd just sit here," Blake said, and he took another swig of his scotch.

"I'm giving you time now," Tyler shouted.

"We don't know who she is. I met her for about two seconds, but I wasn't exactly in the best mood or on my best behavior then. Might I suggest you find out about the little tease?" Byron said.

"What? The two of you are all happy and in committed relationships, so you think my disastrous love live is entertaining?"

Blake guffawed. "Now that you mention it, it is pretty entertaining."

"This is B.S.!"

Tyler marched over to the bar and snagged another beer from the refrigerator. It had been a month since Elena's little stunt and he was still furious. He'd thought he would be over it by now. He'd been determined just to forget all about that … that … never mind.

But a month later he was still dreaming of the wretched woman, still wanting to know what in the hell had gone wrong. More importantly, he was trying to figure out why in the world he gave a damn about any of it. Screw her. Well, he had tried …

"Tyler, you've been going off every few days about this woman since the moment you met her," Byron said. "It's been a few weeks since she walked away from here, and you still haven't forgotten about her. Maybe it's time you to do something about it."

"I wanted to erase her and her effed-up games from my brain," Tyler said, "but you're right. I haven't been able to do that, so I'm thinking that was the wrong choice."

"Haven't you always been the easygoing brother," Blake said, "the happy one, the one who wants to find true love and live all happily ever after?"

"That was before I met the woman before this one, the woman I thought I'd ask to marry me. And now I'm confronted with another wreck, more proof that the female is deadlier than the male," Tyler snapped. "They're all worthless. Who needs them?"

"Don't let one woman, or even two, change your identity," Blake told him. "Byron and I spent far too many years being testosterone-crazed assholes. You're a good guy, Tyler. This woman could be a complete bitch, or she could have a story. You're never going to know if you don't see this thing through, figure out why she did what she did."

"And if I find out that it really was just her idea of a game, that she's actually nothing more than a cheap hussy?"

"*Cheap hussy*? Don't let the tabloids learn that you use that kind of sexist language in this millennium. It won't help our business brand, you know." Byron looked away for a moment, but he continued. "Here's what you do if you find out the worst. You don't let one disastrous encounter — okay, a second disastrous encounter — ruin you for all future women."

"Weren't you being a complete douche to McKenzie just a few months ago?" Tyler had to ask.

"Yeah, I was," Byron admitted with a shake of his head. "And I almost lost her because of it. Don't be an idiot like me."

"Or me," Blake added.

"Dammit! I want to just forget all about this woman."

"Yeah, if life were that easy, there wouldn't be so many damn shrinks out there," Blake said.

"Ha, ha. Very funny," Tyler snapped again.

"Look, bro, all kidding aside, find out this woman's story," Blake told him. "Maybe she's got a damn good reason for doing what she did."

"I can't see that there is any justifiable reason for someone to do what she did," Tyler mumbled. But his temper was finally beginning to die down as he began to plan out his strategy.

"You never know, Ty," Byron said. "In the eyes of the world, you're not exactly a guy bent on monogamy. You're constantly featured in gossip magazines as a playboy extraordinaire. We all went that route. None of us gave a damn what people thought about us. But I'll grant you this — you actually cared about your neighbors, and you've sacrificed to make this world a better place. The same can't be said about Byron or me. We were dicks."

"Hey! I resent that," Byron interjected.

Blake simply raised an eyebrow. And Byron smiled.

"Okay, so I resemble that remark. I *was* a dick. But McKenzie has turned me into a better man."

"Think about it, Ty. All I'm saying is to look a little deeper," Blake told his little brother. "Give peace a chance. You never know what you might find."

"Who in the hell have you guys turned into?" Tyler didn't even recognize these men anymore. "Wasn't I always the voice of reason in our trio?"

"Yeah. The right woman happened to each of us. The love of our life." Blake didn't even bat an eye at saying this.

Tyler couldn't help but goad his brothers. "So you've gone soft?"

Blake sat up and the look of a warrior sprang into his eyes, the same look that could silence a boardroom and make people shake.

"Just because my heart has softened doesn't make me weak. Don't for one second think that's the case. I just came to realize that I don't have to be alone and miserable in this world. If someone crosses me, I'm still a force to be reckoned with."

"How do you separate it?" Tyler asked. He didn't feel quite so angry now.

"You learn to adjust, to figure out what's worth getting upset about, and what's not," Byron said. "Sometimes you slip up, but you forgive yourself."

"Thank you."

They sat there a few more moments and then his brothers said goodbye. Maybe they were right. Maybe he was a fool, but since he couldn't get this woman off his mind, he might as well find out why that was.

The games with one Elena Truman weren't quite over yet.

CHAPTER SIXTEEN

"ELENA, GET IN here!"

Ugh. Sometimes Elena really hated her boss. Seriously. He was arrogant and condescending. Okay, so he was also brilliant, and he brought in clients. And though she loathed him, she needed this job. It wasn't easy to get a job with decent pay right out of law school, and every law school grad was enough in debt from student loans to … oh, use your own cliché here. She had a long way to go before she could do what she truly loved, which was helping children. She only got to do that now on a volunteer basis, and with her long hours, her time for that was incredibly limited.

It was good that she had a job, and one that wasn't the worst in the world, because the rest of her life was an utter disaster. Her revenge plan had left her miserable. She'd never expected to miss Tyler Knight, had expected to feel triumphant and righteous, but miss him she did. Every single day — and night. Especially night.

They'd spent time together for only a month, a single month, but that time with him had brought the past back to her like a hurricane. There was a brief moment in her life when Tyler had been her best friend, and while she'd been executing her plan, she'd seen glimpses of the boy she'd once loved so much.

She had to remind herself that he was now a man she despised for justifiable reasons. But it was difficult sometimes.

Picking up her iPad in case her boss wanted her to take down some notes, she stepped into his office and waited while he finished speaking on the phone. The man was rude, too. Obviously.

"We have a new client, and he's requested you, for some odd reason. I did tell him that we have attorneys here who have a longer track record and could do the job better."

Elena gritted her teeth and kept silent. She was good at her job. Sure, she'd only been practicing law for a couple of years or so, but she was dedicated, worked long hours, and took great care of her clients.

"Don't you have anything to say?" asked her boss, Timothy. "I'm giving you a great case."

"I do appreciate it. Just give me the file and I'll begin reviewing it immediately."

"No file yet. The client wants to meet you face-to-face first and then discuss the case. You'll meet with him tonight — eight o'clock at the Fairmont Hotel, in the Georgian restaurant."

"Okay, I'll be there." That was unusual — not to have notes to go over first. Most clients wanted their attorneys up and running on any case before they wasted their time and money on talking.

She turned to leave Timothy's office when he called out her name and she stopped and turned around.

"Elena, give this man whatever he wants. This is a high-profile client with megabucks in the bank and in the stock market."

Dammit! She loathed clients like this.

There was nothing unusual about meeting a client at night, but she hated the ones who had a lot of demands. Still, many of her practice's clients were incredibly busy, and her job certainly wasn't an eight-to-five kind of gig. She'd enjoyed some of the dinner meetings with clients at exclusive places that she couldn't usually afford. The problem was finding something to wear that would be appropriate at a restaurant such as the Georgian.

But she'd become pretty good at faking it, and she could stretch her dollars better than most.

Work ate up the rest of Elena's day, and though not having a file so she could study up on her client first didn't make her happy, sometimes that's just how the job went. So she went home and rustled up a nice black pencil skirt, not too short, and a blue top that matched her eyes.

After throwing her hair into a tight bun and touching up her make-up, she nodded into her bathroom mirror.

With time to spare, she caught a cab to the Fairmont and walked inside. Her heels clicked on the marble floor as she proceeded to the Georgian.

When she gave her name to the host, she didn't have to wait at all. He escorted her back to the restaurant's private dining room, *The Petite*, a room she certainly hadn't seen before. As Elena made her way past the other diners, live music drifted through the room.

She was a little disappointed that she wouldn't be sitting out there where she could listen. But this was a business meeting. She'd have to suck it up. The story of her life. And it definitely sucked.

When Elena entered the private room, she saw that her client hadn't yet arrived, so she took a seat and ordered an iced tea. She normally had a glass of wine at dinners of this sort, but she knew nothing about this client or about what he wanted.

Normally, this would be fine if she had the dang case file. Then at least she wouldn't be sitting there doing nothing when the man entered. Her firm took pride in the fact that they were sought after, on top of things.

Unsure whether she should check her phone or sit there and pretend to be in deep thought, she began to grow antsy when the atmosphere in the room suddenly changed.

Elena didn't need to turn around, didn't need to make eye contact to know who had joined her. Maybe she was going to need that wine after all.

CHAPTER SEVENTEEN

"**Y**OU LOOK GOOD, Elena," Tyler said as he stepped in front of her. He looked good too. He was wearing a dark gray suit and a red tie, his coat pushed open to reveal the crisp white shirt beneath and the hand-tailored trousers showcasing his magnificent hips. His hair was neat and his face clean-shaven, and a predator's smile — not unlike the one she'd seen in his bedroom a month ago — rested on his lips. She didn't want to find him sexy, but it was incredibly hard not to.

"Thank you," she gritted out, thinking over and over again that she had to be nice or risk losing her job. Tyler knew this and was thoroughly enjoying himself.

"I figured out a lot of things about you in the last month. You should be impressed with yourself. You managed to intrigue me, and that's more than I can say about most people."

"Such a self-absorbed remark, Tyler. Is that what I should be impressed about?" she asked. "And I *wasn't* trying to intrigue you."

"What were you trying to do, then, Elena?"

He sat down in the chair across from her. His legs brushed against hers beneath the table and she scooted back. He just smiled and extended his leg, and his foot was now toying with hers. She was going to be gritting her teeth a lot during this meal.

"It doesn't matter what I was trying to do," she said before taking a breath. This wasn't going to get them anywhere. "Can we get directly to business?"

"Tsk, tsk, Elena. You aren't being very hospitable right now," he said. "Especially since we know each other quite … intimately."

Elena took a few deep breaths and unclenched her teeth before responding. "This is a business meeting. Let's be professionals and focus on *business* only," she said in her best prim voice.

"Yes, business. How is Timothy?"

"My boss?" she said somewhat confused by the quick change in conversation. He nodded. "He's fine. Though I don't know how you managed to convince him not to give me your name. If I'd been better prepared, then we wouldn't be wasting your time at six hundred dollars an hour."

"I'm the client. If I tell your boss I want to keep my name anonymous until I'm ready to give it, then that's exactly what he'll do," Tyler said before leaning forward. "As a matter of fact, he will do anything I ask of him because he's a smart man and knows not to antagonize me."

Elena gasped at his audacity. "Who in the hell do you think you are?" Screw this job!

"I thought you knew exactly who I am, Elena. Isn't that why you decided to come after me with everything you had?"

The gleam in his eyes reminded her of a hungry tiger. And Elena had no doubt that she was now his prey.

"You're clearly not a very savvy businessman. Do you even need an attorney, Tyler?"

Her shoulders back, Elena didn't break eye contact. If she showed him an ounce of weakness right now, he'd go right for the jugular. There was no use in making his kill any easier by exposing her throat to him.

"Yes, I have a number of attorneys for a number of purposes. I need a new one now."

"For what exactly?" she asked.

"You will find out, won't you?"

"This is about payback, isn't it? I played a game with you, and now it's your turn," Elena said.

He was quiet for several moments and then he smiled, though the expression didn't quite make it to his eyes. He was certainly playing with her, and he wasn't even trying to hide it. When he spoke next, she could barely keep up with his change in voice or topic.

"I've had a very good day so far. I went to a job site with my brother Blake, had a nice lunch, and met with your boss. I'm feeling very relaxed. You don't want to ruin my day now by making unfounded accusations, do you, Elena?"

Oh, he was so damn smooth, so cocky. How had she ever thought she'd be able to go up against a man like him and win? It was impossible. The world was made up of the haves and have-nots. She was a have-not. He was most certainly a have. So she was screwed from the get-go.

"I apologize if anything I've said or done tonight has somehow made you uncomfortable," she said, though it took a lot out of her to say the words. Did she really like her job? She could work somewhere else, surely.

Then again, he was the sort of man who would just follow her wherever she went. She'd ticked the man off and he was bound and determined to work up his own revenge plot. So she might as well accept it and hope he grew bored before he made all of her life go up in smoke.

"You know that you and I will become lovers, don't you?"

He said the words so casually that it took a moment for her brain to process them. When they did, her cheeks flushed, partly with anger and partly with excitement. She'd had a taste of what being Tyler Knight's lover felt like, and that taste hadn't been unpleasant. In fact, it had been too damn good.

"No, Mr. Knight, we will not be lovers," she told him in ringing tones — right before the waiter approached. *Not again,* she added silently.

How mortifying — the waiter had to have heard her unfortunate comment. She couldn't look him in the eyes, so she stared down at the menu instead.

"What's your preference in wine?"

That Tyler had bothered to ask surprised Elena. She'd just assumed he was the type of man to make all the decisions. Or to try to, anyway.

"I like light white wines," she told him. She didn't add, however, that the bottles she bought always cost less than ten dollars. "Though isn't it taboo to choose a wine before you know what dish it's to be paired with? Doesn't that count as an extreme crime against social order?"

Tyler laughed at her words. "Then I guess we'll rebel against the rules tonight." He made his choice from the wine menu and sent the waiter on his way to find the bottle.

"Mr. Knight —"

He interrupted her with his patented quirk of the eyebrows. "I'm *Mr. Knight* now?"

"Yes, you are," she said firmly.

"Hmm. It's kind of erotic coming from your lips, Elena."

Dammit! It didn't seem that she could say anything at the moment without his answering with some sort of sexual innuendo. Hell, that didn't even count as innuendo. Too blatant.

"Really, we should get down to business, Mr. Knight. I don't want to waste your time or your money."

"*Get down* to business? Nice idea. In any case, I'm not in a hurry," he told her. "And I have plenty of money."

Pig. She was most certainly in a hurry to get away from him. She almost said so. But discretion won out. "Why don't you tell me exactly what you're going to be needing me for?"

The waiter brought in their wine and some appetizers, and that briefly interrupted their conversation. When the fellow left, Tyler spoke.

"There's plenty of time for you to figure that out. I will say, though, that our work together will last for several months — at least until I don't find a use for you any longer."

Elena was dead silent for several heartbeats. He was letting her know in no uncertain terms that they were playing by his rules now.

"As always, the gentleman," she told him. "I'm sure you can easily find a lawyer far more qualified than I am." She couldn't put on a performance for months. No freaking way.

"*You* are the woman I want."

Elena felt trapped. She wasn't normally subject to claustrophobia, and the room, though private, was hardly small, but it seemed to be closing in on her. This couldn't possibly work.

"Until you get your payback, right, Tyler?" She was so flustered that she'd used his first name.

He sat back, his head tilted slightly to one side as he gazed at her with something in his eyes that she couldn't read. Maybe he just enjoyed throwing her off kilter. Maybe, just maybe, if she didn't react, he'd stop. Maybe.

"Payback? Maybe. Punishment? — that would be a nice idea … if I were into bondage. Hmm …" He paused as if to consider it, then shook his head and continued. "No, I don't need special kinks to get me off." Tyler lifted his wineglass as if to offer a toast, and then he took a sip. "I'm enjoying this relationship, I must say."

"We aren't in a relationship," she almost growled.

"I disagree. I think we've been in a relationship since that little episode on my kitchen island," he said, reaching across the table and taking her hand before she could move it out of the way.

Her words became stuck in her throat as he lifted her hand to his lips and began kissing her palm, then each of her fingers, acting like a lover. Damn if what he was doing didn't feel incredible.

Could a person both loathe and desire a man so desperately at the same time? It seemed a definite possibility. Hell — more than a possibility.

"So you're bent on destroying me," Elena said.

Tyler stopped kissing her hand but didn't release it. She dug her fingernails into his palm, but at first that had no effect. When he finally let go, all he did was rise from his chair and move to the seat next to her. And he quickly took her hand again, though she tried to move it out of his way. A shudder passed through her when he rested their joined fingers high up on his thigh.

"I don't know where this game will end for us, Elena," he practically purred. "But I will tell you that my main goal is pleasure — pleasure you owe me. We will finish what we started. And I suspect that it will be a hell of a ride." He leaned closer, and his lips were now only half an inch from hers. "Kiss me now."

She nearly did exactly that, but she stopped herself a millimeter before their lips touched.

"I'm not doing this."

"You *will*, and you'll enjoy it."

"You might think that I should be flattered that you find me worth your interest, but I'm not flattered at all. I want no part of this game of yours."

"Yes, you do, Elena. I know how much you love to play games," he said. "And I also know how much you want me. You're doing a lousy job at hiding it."

"Look, Tyler. I'm sorry, okay? I should have known that I couldn't possibly win. My game was foolish, and I regret it."

"The game has only begun, Elena. You started it, and I will finish it. There's nothing you can do at this point that will cause me to lose interest."

"I was putting on a show, Tyler. I'm not that girl you met at the bar last month." She let her hand go limp in his. "That girl doesn't exist."

"I can find her again," he said with a wolfish smile.

Elena started casting about in her brain for any way to make this guy run off in terror. She had to. Ah! She just had to bore him to death. That shouldn't be too hard. She wasn't as fascinating as he seemed to think. She worked, spent time with her best friend, then worked some more. She devoted most of her weekends to working or volunteering. Piece of cake. Just being herself would drive this man away.

"Did you know that the government poisoned alcohol during Prohibition, killing at least ten thousand people?"

Tyler looked at her with confusion. "What are you talking about?"

"And did you know that a hundred acres of pizza are served daily in the United States?"

Tyler laughed before he pushed his chair a bit closer to hers, brushing his leg against her.

"It won't work, Elena," he whispered.

"Wh … what won't work?" she gasped as his lips made contact with her neck. She really hoped he didn't notice her leaping pulse.

"Spouting random facts, trying to bore me. I can bring out the naughty girl in no time at all. You want me. You can deny it all you want, deny it to yourself and to me, but I've got your number, if I may be a little trite."

Before she could respond, he took hold of the back of her neck and kissed her, not in a quick meeting of the mouths, but in a kiss that was full of possession and passion.

When he pulled back, her body was on fire and she was glad she was sitting down, because her legs had turned to jelly. She wasn't going to survive this — certainly not for months, if she had to work for him that long. She didn't think she could even survive more than today.

She had no defenses against this man.

And he knew it.

CHAPTER EIGHTEEN

"... INSUFFERABLE ..."
"... jackass ..."
"... low-down ... dirty rotten ..."

Elena had been storming around their tiny living room for the past hour, ranting and raving while her best friend and roommate sat on the couch and occupied herself, now and then, by munching on tortilla chips. Each time her friend smiled, Elena shot her a dirty look, which wiped the smile away, but only briefly. Piper clearly didn't understand how serious this situation was.

"Aren't you going to say anything? I've been talking forever and I'm looking for advice," Elena said, hands on her hips.

"Oh, is it my turn to speak now?" Piper asked.

"I've given you plenty of time to talk. You've just been sitting there with your junk food, not a care in the world."

Piper laughed. "You've been ranting nonstop, darling. I think it's great, but, no, you haven't let me speak yet."

"Well, I'm giving you a chance now."

"Do you want my honest opinion?"

"Maybe I don't," Elena replied. "The way you asked that question isn't exactly inspiring me."

"Too bad. I'm your best friend, and sometimes that calls for tough love," Piper told her.

"Fine. Give it to me." Elena was suddenly tired as her rage dimmed.

She sat down on the far end of the couch from Piper, though the couch wasn't all that big.

"I think you like this guy — really, *really* like this guy."

Elena waited for more, but Piper was silent after saying the stupidest thing ever.

"That's ridiculous, Piper. I've just been going off — in great detail, I might add — on what I despise about him."

"Yeah, sure. But I have a minor remark about that. We don't usually get so passionate about people who don't interest us."

"This isn't passion," Elena said. "This is fury. Fury that he's forcing me to work with him."

"You could always tell your boss there's a conflict of interest with this client … because he's had your legs wide open on his kitchen counter while he was doing naughty, naughty things to you with his evil tongue."

Elena hit her own head violently with one hand. "I knew I never should have told you about that. But I don't throw *your* mistakes into your face, Piper."

"That's a lie and we both know it. If we can't mock the ones we love, then who in the hell can we have fun with?"

"Ugh! This has just gotten so dang complicated." Elena sagged down and threw her arm over her face.

"Of course it's complicated, you drama queen. You tried to punish your old best friend from a million years ago, the guy who'd also taken your virginity several years later. That same man also comes from a wickedly bad family, and he's now become a very wealthy man who is sexy as hell. It was complicated the second you decided to carry out a revenge plot after having a little too much to drink."

"Okay, so I'm impulsive and I have a temper. Once I decide on something, I have to see it through, though. You know that."

"Yeah, that's called *stubborn*, darling, no matter how you sugarcoat it. Revenge isn't so sweet after all, is it?"

"You could at least pretend that you're on my side," Elena said.

"I'm always on your side. You know that. If you kill this man, I'm your gal. I will help you hide the body and give you an alibi."

Elena finally smiled for the first time in hours, ever since that long and awkward dinner with Tyler. "I would do the same for you," she said.

"Good, that's the Elena I want to hear from, not the crazy girl," Piper told her. "What are we going to do about this situation?"

"I'm going to quit my job."

"We both know that's not going to happen, so what are you really going to do?"

"I don't know. Avoid the hell out of him. Maybe if I'm careful to stay at least three feet away from him at all times, my boneheaded hormones won't take over."

"*Boneheaded*? How Freudian of you. I see where your thoughts really are. You know, you could just get it over with and stay in bed for forty-eight hours straight. Maybe that would get him out of your system. In and out of your system, so to speak."

"Don't put thoughts like that in my head," Elena said. "I hate the man."

"Are you sure about that? I'm not. I think you want his body so badly that you're melting down. I've wanted a few guys that much. It's too damn bad that I did nothing about it. Now it's Friday night and I'm stuck home with you instead of getting down and dirty with some hot stud."

"Piper, you talk a hell of a game, but you're about as experienced in the bedroom as I am."

"Well, I have a much more vivid imagination than you do," Piper said. "We both know that."

"Of course you do. You're a *librarian*," Elena told her with an epic eye roll.

"Which is why I can never meet any hot studs. You know what they say about sex in the stacks? Stirring up the dust and all that? Well, it never happens. I make a point of going there at least once every shift and I've yet to get ravished." Piper let out an elaborate sigh.

"One of these days I'm going to hire some serious hottie. He'll be waiting back there with a video camera set up, and then I'll use the expression on your face for blackmail for the rest of your life."

"Oh, puh-lease, Elena. If I found a hot stud back there, I so wouldn't give you a second thought. I'd just rip off my clothes and pounce on him. Jump his proverbial bones. Or bone, but definitely more than once."

"You've been reading far too many romance novels," Elena said. "Maybe you should stick with the classics."

Piper smiled. She'd effectively pulled her friend out of that grumpy mood, just as she'd known she would. That's what friends were for, even if it sometimes took a while.

"And you need to answer your phone the next time that man calls you," Piper said. She shot a pointed look at Elena's cell, which had buzzed several times in the last hour.

"Nope. I'm off duty on the weekends — at least when it comes to Tyler Knight."

"*Comes*? Interesting word choice, as usual. But I thought he was a primo client that you had to make happy."

"I'll just say my phone died if I'm asked about it. He never told me I had to be available for anything this weekend. Where's the bottle of wine?"

"I'm so on that," Piper said. She leapt up and ran to the kitchen, immediately pulling out a bottle from the refrigerator and filling two glasses.

"Thanks! Let's get plastered," Elena told her, "maybe eat some popcorn with a lot of butter on it, and forget all about men, at least for two days."

"If you can go fifteen minutes without saying a word about Tyler, I'll believe you hate the guy," Piper said as she popped a movie into the DVD player. "Or I might."

After another hour and two bottles of wine, Elena had interrupted the film roughly a dozen times to grumble about Tyler. The knowing looks that Piper was sending her way weren't reassuring, and she was thinking that maybe it was time to call it a night. Piper would never believer that she didn't want Tyler.

Hell, she'd never believe it herself.

CHAPTER NINETEEN

JUGGLING THE DRINKS and a sack carrying their sandwiches, Elena pushed her way into the library, and went to the back, where Piper was waiting for her.

When she heard quiet laughter, she stopped. That voice sounded familiar, but what in the world would he be doing at Piper's workplace? And why would Piper be laughing? She stopped and gulped in some air. It was most likely just someone who sounded like Tyler. Since the man was constantly on her mind, it had to be her imagination.

Unfreezing, she moved forward and turned the corner to find Tyler and Piper both sitting at the table in the library break room. Both of them wore silly grins.

"What are you doing here?" Elena's tone wasn't friendly.

"I work here," Piper said, deliberately intercepting the question as she rose and grabbed the bag from Elena.

Sending an irritated look her friend's way, she then turned to Tyler, who didn't appear in the least apologetic for being there.

"I had to check out a book and ran into Piper here. We've been talking for a while now. Your friend has a vast knowledge of business procedures," Tyler said, and he kicked back in the chair as if he didn't plan to go anywhere in the near future.

"I'm here now, so you can leave."

Tyler's eyes narrowed the slightest bit.

"Well, since we've managed to run into each other and I haven't been able to get you on the phone, I think now is a good time to discuss business."

"Do you normally stalk your attorneys?"

She didn't want to allow him to set a precedent of showing up any time he felt like it at places that were her stomping grounds. But it appeared that Tyler Knight, as always, would do whatever the hell he pleased.

"I do business wherever I feel like it. I didn't become as successful as I have by sticking with convention."

They had a stare-off for several moments, during which Elena was sure the library heated up a few degrees.

Then Piper interrupted. "I'm going to have lunch. Are you guys joining me?"

Elena wasn't thrilled that her best friend was entertaining the man who was driving her insane, but she quickly quashed that sentiment. What should Piper have done? Tell him to go away? That sounded much easier than it was. The guy didn't listen. He'd stopped doing that when he hit puberty — most likely before, actually.

"If we're going to meet, we might as well eat. I'm hungry," Elena finally said.

"Good. Me too." Piper grabbed her sandwich and kicked back, pretending she didn't notice the tension brewing.

Elena sat in the seat across from Tyler. At least this table was too wide for him to try to play footsies with her. She didn't think she could handle him touching her at the moment. Her nerves were scraped too raw.

"I can't finish this whole thing. Do you want half?" Piper asked.

"Thanks. Don't mind if I do," Tyler replied, ever so polite.

"What do you want to discuss?" Elena asked while slowly unwrapping her sandwich. She'd felt as if she were starving. Now she couldn't seem to find her appetite.

"We can eat first, then talk later," he said, seeming content to munch on the turkey and Swiss.

"Fine by me. I've started your billing from the moment I sat down."

"Why don't we just call it an even eight hours today? That way you won't get anxious," he said, taking a bite and sitting back without a care in the world.

"I've got a full schedule," Elena pointed out. "I don't plan on meeting with you for eight hours."

"You never know where things will lead," he said right back.

Her friend was whipping her head back and forth between the two of them, and Elena sent her a silent plea for help.

Piper smiled. "Do you need me to leave so you two can just get it on right here in the library?"

Elena gasped. Tyler looked thoughtful for a moment before giving Piper his award-winning smile.

"I have heard rumors about the stacks," he said with a wink.

Elena turned red before ducking her head. She didn't know which person she was more irritated with at the moment — Piper or Tyler.

"You both should keep your voices down. We are, after all, in a library," she snapped.

"Yes, but it's slow today," Piper said. "Talk all you want."

Tyler finished his sandwich and then rose from the table. With wary eyes, Elena watched him move over to the trash can and throw away his garbage before moving back over to the table and taking the seat next to her.

What in the heck was he up to now?

"So," Piper asked him, "what have you been doing that is making my best friend all antsy?"

Tyler threw her a smile before shifting in the chair and brushing his leg against Elena. Elena refused to move. If she showed this man the effect he was having on her, then he'd win. He liked winning.

So did she.

The problem was that where he touched her, little fingers of delight shot through her body. And from the look her best friend was shooting her way, Piper clearly knew exactly what was going on across the table from her.

Dammit!

"I plan on being her lover," Tyler said.

Elena gasped at his audacity. "You seriously have no bounds, do you, Tyler?"

"No. I figure it's best to tell it like it is. That way there will be no mis-understandings between us."

"There's definitely a misunderstanding between us. I don't plan to get anywhere near a bed with you."

"I never said it had to be on a bed, Elena."

"And how isn't this sexual harassment?" Elena asked with a glare.

Tyler paused as his lips turned up. Then he leaned closer to her, his breath fanning the side of her face and neck. For once Piper was silent, though Elena would really have liked it if her friend had spoken up and broken this tension.

"Do you want to file a complaint? I know an excellent attorney."

Elena wasn't normally a violent person — lawyers had to be careful, after all — but she had to resist the urge to give some action to her fingernails.

Piper spoke up. "What exactly is Elena doing for you? I meant that in a work-related sense. The rest is obvious."

Tyler turned his attention to her best friend, and Elena let out the breath she hadn't realized she was holding.

"I have several projects going on right now," he said. "There's plenty of work for Elena."

"That doesn't really tell me anything." Piper wasn't one to mince words, thankfully.

Elena was also eager to know what she was doing for Tyler. Right now, he didn't seem to need her services at all — well, at least not her legal services.

"She's offered her ... let's say ... impressive skills to help me out," Tyler responded.

His meaning was loud and clear, and Elena felt her cheeks heat even though she'd done nothing of the sort. She wasn't his personal call girl, wasn't available for the services he was insinuating that she was there for.

"Hmm. Don't underestimate my best friend. She's skilled in more ways than you know," Piper said with a wink.

Elena was so shocked that she almost choked. What strange alternate universe had she fallen into? She understood this from Tyler. He was a dog. But her best friend? Had aliens overtaken her body?

"Yes, I'm quite aware of her skills," Tyler said. "We've been dating for a month now."

"She *has* been gone a lot lately. And she's been so secretive. Are you the reason she's been so tired?"

Before Tyler could say anything, Elena jumped in. "Sorry to say this, Piper, but I *have* been home. You've been the one gone so much. Maybe you've been hiding some secrets of your own."

If she turned the tables, maybe this inquisition would stop. Please, please ...

"Your life is so much more interesting than mine," Piper said, not falling for the bait. "I've been working at the library and helping my brother out with his business because he's short-staffed. Nothing interesting there."

"How long have you been a librarian, Piper?" Tyler asked.

"About five years," she said.

He paused at that. "Well, you're not like Mrs. Pokey, my old high school librarian," he said with a laugh.

"And why is that, Tyler?"

Elena sat back. She wanted to see how Tyler dug himself out of this. Piper hated it when people put down her job. Yes, her best friend was beautiful, but she was also brilliant. The girl hated it when people assumed she was stupid because a person couldn't have brains and looks.

"I picture librarians as little old ladies with big glasses and permanent scowls," he said.

"Maybe that's because you're sexist and into old stereotypes," Piper told him, "and don't read all that much. I guess you pay people to look everything up for you."

"Not at all," he said. "I might have to start reading for pleasure again if you're the new example of librarians."

Piper laughed, much to Elena's dismay. "You're quite smooth, Tyler. Not. I think you're far more bark than bite, though. Do you mean all these things you say, or do you just enjoy getting a reaction?"

"You say what you want, don't you, Piper?"

"I've never found it productive to sneak around words. If you want answers, you're far better off just asking the right questions."

"Good. Then what will it take to get your best friend in my bed?"

That question was followed by a moment of silence. Tyler had shocked Piper, and Elena was too horrified to say anything.

Finally, Piper smiled, and Elena's stomach sank.

"First of all, you have to make it past her best friend," Piper told him.

"And do you approve?" he asked.

She smiled again, and Elena watched as the two of them bonded right in front of her.

"You're growing on me."

"Well, neither one of you is growing on me," Elena said.

"Tsk, tsk, Elena. It's not good to lie," Tyler told her.

"I'm done with this."

Elena rose from the table, shot both of them a dirty look, and stormed away.

This would be so much easier if she really did hate the man. But she didn't. She only wanted to. And being stuck with him wasn't making her life any easier.

CHAPTER TWENTY

WHEN ELENA'S DOORBELL rang late on Saturday night, she jumped and set her book aside. She had no doubt who was at the door.

Ignoring Tyler's calls apparently wasn't working as she'd hoped it would. But it was okay. She'd just say she'd gone to bed early, apologize for the phone problems, and promise to do her best to help him out — when Monday morning came around.

After the disastrous library meeting on Tuesday, she'd managed to confine their meetings to public places, and then Friday night had come and she'd turned off her phone. She could only take so much of the man.

Ranting and raving about him all week to Piper hadn't done her any good either. Piper was convinced that Elena was lying to herself, that she needed to just sleep with the man again and then either marry him or dump him.

Piper didn't know what she was talking about.

After switching off her bedside lamp, Elena tucked herself beneath her covers, with her head securely under her pillow.

She'd been watching romantic movies all day — stupid move — and then she'd soaked in a hot bath. The way the water glided over her breasts, dammit, had made her think about sex — sex with one Tyler Knight.

She heard the front door open and then voices.

Piper was home early. She'd been driving for her brother earlier, so Elena had thought she was safe, that no one would answer Tyler's knock.

Footsteps sounded outside in the hallway and Elena found herself holding her breath. She could pretend to be asleep and hopefully the two of them would go away. Heck, Tyler and Piper got along great. Maybe the two of them would hook up.

Why was that thought so incredibly depressing?

"Elena, you have a visitor," Piper called through the doorway.

"I'm trying to sleep," Elena called back, which was *so* stupid — now they knew she was awake.

"Coming in."

That was her only warning before her door was thrust open and her light flipped on.

"Look who I found on our doorstep. He insisted on seeing you. Since you're *never* in bed this early, I figured you wouldn't mind."

Piper gave her a wink behind Tyler's back, then made a kissy-face before she turned and left. *The traitor!*

"You've been avoiding me, Elena," Tyler said, moving confidently into her room. He looked around, and she felt herself blushing as she tried to see if anything was out of place.

Of course things were. It was her *bed*room.

He moved over to her favorite chair, a dark green stuffed armchair that had seen better days, but was the most comfortable piece of furniture she owned. And he picked up the nightie she had hanging on the back.

The look he sent her had her blushing and sputtering at the same time.

"Don't touch my stuff," she snapped. She wanted to jump out of the bed, but the nightie she was wearing was even more minuscule than the one he had in his hot hands. Not the sort of thing to parade around in front of a man she wasn't going to have sex with.

"I like it," he said. "Do you always wear silky little nighties? And what are you wearing now?"

"None of your business."

He looked at her comforter as if he could see through it, and that made her clutch the thing tightly.

"It smells marvelous in here. Are you burning a candle?"

"I did earlier, but then I decided to go to sleep," she growled.

"At …" He looked down at his watch, then looked back at her. "… Nine on a Saturday night?"

"It's none of your business when I do or don't go to bed, Tyler. And your presence in my bedroom is a clear invasion of privacy. You're trespassing."

"Do you have any idea how sexy you look right now with your hair rumpled, the top of your nightie dipping deliciously low, and your eyes spitting fire?"

Dang. She hadn't realized that her comforter had slipped down. She tugged harder on it.

"This is so not appropriate," she gasped. If only she'd been able to say that with some sort of force.

"When will you realize that there isn't a question here? We're going to be together, and that's indisputable. You have nothing to feel guilty about by wanting me."

"I don't feel guilty, and I have no idea why you think I do."

"You've been lying to me since we met, and whether you want to admit it or not, you still are."

If she didn't stop this now, she didn't know how far it would go. Her raging hormones weren't doing her a lick of good. Ugh! She didn't need to think about him and licking in the same train of thought.

"Look, Tyler. I told you I screwed up. I'm sorry I got you hot and bothered and walked out. I'm trying to move forward now, and I won't do anything like that again. Can't you please just request another attorney, one who can give you far more time?"

"No. I think you're the most qualified person for what I have in mind."

The man had no qualms, no interest in hiding how he felt or what he expected. Yes, this was a clear invasion of her privacy, or her professionalism, of her life, but her boss wouldn't care. And what she'd done with Tyler already — more precisely, what she'd let him do to her — didn't exactly put her in the best light. The statute of limitations on what had happened when she was twenty had run out.

It took her a minute to find her voice. "This is insane, Tyler. You have to realize that."

"I don't think so. I decided I liked what you started back in the bar," he said with a wolfish smile. "And I want to keep on playing. Once you start something involving others, the decision to say when it ends is no longer yours alone."

"What do you expect from me?"

He stood up very, very slowly, and she forgot to breathe when he moved toward her and stood at the foot of her bed, all six-plus feet of him, all breathtaking, all intoxicating male. He leaned down, and she scooted back, using the precious few inches she had.

"I expect *us* to see this through," he said.

His voice aroused her in ways she hadn't known were possible.

"Why?" she gulped.

He threw her a look that she couldn't quite interpret, and he was silent for several heart-stopping moments. Finally, she remembered to take in a much-needed breath of air.

"You don't see it, do you?" he said.

Now it was her turn to be silent for a moment. Then, when she spoke, she wasn't even sure he could hear her, her voice was so quiet.

"See what?"

He walked around to the side of her bed and got even closer. Damn, he smelled incredible.

"You're mine, Elena. I've wanted you from the moment we met in that bar. I tried to fight it, but some things are fated. Why are *you* fighting it?"

"I … uh …" She couldn't complete her thought. Or even start it.

"Why not finish this, Elena? Neither of us is seeing anyone else right now. As the newspapers might say, a good time could be had by all."

She almost threw off her covers and held out her arms to him. But the logical side of her knew this had to be a new twist on the game-playing between them.

Was he going for payback? Would he get her all aroused and desperate and then turn and walk away? She'd deserve it. But there was a big difference between the two of them. He had an ego the size of Alaska, and hers was fragile. She didn't handle rejection well. She definitely hadn't done so when she was ten years old or when she was twenty, and she wasn't that much stronger now.

Her fears gave her the strength to stiffen her spine and throw him a withering look.

"I don't think so, Tyler. Yes, maybe I do feel … some small glimmer of something when I'm around you, but not enough to compromise myself."

He smiled — the man actually smiled as he leaned back just a little bit.

"You'll change your mind, Elena. I guarantee it," he said before straightening up. But only for a moment. Instead of walking out her door, he sat down on the side of her bed.

"What are you doing?"

She was clutching the comforter so tightly now that she knew her fingers were going to cramp up at any minute. But it was worth it. It kept her from reaching for him.

"Just giving you something to think about, Elena."

He leaned down and gripped her head. Before she was able to utter a word, his mouth covered hers. Tyler traced her lips and then dived in as if he owned her.

Each stroke of his tongue sent tiny messages throughout her body, begging her to let him give her what she really wanted. The voice inside her head telling her that this was an awful idea was growing further and further away.

And then he released her.

"Self-sacrifice doesn't do you any good, Elena. You will hurt all night — I guarantee it."

He rose up and strode from her room.

It took her a good half hour before she could control the ache that he'd left behind. He was right. She was going to hurt the rest of the night, and maybe for a lot longer. She turned off the lights, then tossed and turned for the next hour.

Then a message came in on her cell phone, the one she'd told him was off, but was merely on vibration mode.

I'll pick you up at six Monday evening — for work. Sweet dreams.

She wanted to toss her phone across the room and shatter it. She hated him, yes — for sure it was hate. She wanted to go and yell at Piper for letting the man in. But she decided against that.

She would prove Tyler wrong and sleep like a baby, she told herself.

No such luck.

CHAPTER TWENTY-ONE

B Y MONDAY MORNING, Elena was feeling grouchy, to say the least, from lack of sleep. She hadn't heard another word from Tyler, but that didn't mean the man hadn't been on her mind constantly from the time he'd walked out of her bedroom a day and a half earlier.

She'd even gone running on Sunday, jogging through a nearby park until her legs were weak and she barely had the energy to step into the shower and wash the sweat off. And she still hadn't managed to nod off for very long.

Yes, she wanted him, and she was sure that much was obvious. But a long line of women had to be lusting after Tyler Knight. Or at least interested enough in his money to try to lure him into the sack. Why couldn't he just run off and play with one of those little bimbos?

That thought sent a pang right through her, though she fought to convince herself that she really did want that easy way out of this mess. She just didn't want to hear about it or see it.

Amid all her work on legal briefs and on contracts — she was going at it all double-time — she wondered what they were meeting about tonight. If he planned to monopolize all her evenings through the course of this project, she was going to be very, very cranky by the time it ended. She had to struggle through a boatload of paperwork during the day, and everyone deserved private time. Yes, her company got to bill him for every hour he was with her, but that didn't change how much she actually made, and it wasn't much, not when she was paying off her student loans.

When Elena dashed home, she changed into something a little more comfortable — this time it was slacks, because there was no way she'd wear another skirt around that guy, and she put on a thick sweater, which was making her too warm already. By the time she did that her doorbell was already ringing. Would the pressure never let up?

She answered it reluctantly, expecting to find Tyler standing there. She was faced instead with a stranger wearing a suit.

"May I help you?"

"I'm here to give you a ride, Ms. Truman," the man answered.

"I'm not sure I need a ride," she said slowly.

"Mr. Knight sent me."

The guy didn't look like a serial killer, but how was she to know what a serial killer actually looked like? Even people with law degrees weren't always that clued in. And she rarely touched criminal law.

"Can you wait out there for a moment?" she asked. He nodded and she shut her door before moving over to her cell phone and sending out a quick text.

Tyler immediately responded that, yes, it was his driver, and that he, Tyler, looked forward to seeing her. Well, she wasn't looking forward to seeing him.

Gritting her teeth, Elena grabbed her purse, went back to her front door, and followed the driver to the black SUV waiting at the curb.

When the driver pulled up to the gate to Tyler's house, she was instantly tense all over again. He'd neglected to tell her the meeting was at his place. How convenient for him!

It wouldn't do her any good to yell at his driver. The man was just doing his job. But she'd give Tyler an earful when she got inside.

But as the driver let her in through the front door, she rethought that. What good would it do? Tyler was her client, and no matter where he wanted the meetings, she had to deal with it — and they both knew it. Why waste her breath?

"Mr. Knight can be found this way," the driver said before leading her back into the kitchen.

The freaking kitchen? Who in this world held business meetings in the kitchen? She really didn't want to go in there.

Of course her eyes were immediately drawn to the damn kitchen island the second they stepped into the room. When she met Tyler's gaze after a moment of staring at that miserable spot, she couldn't miss the victory in his eyes. He knew exactly what she was thinking about.

Despite her outrage at what the guy was pulling, she felt her body respond, her nipples instantly hardening — thank goodness for the thick sweater — and her core heating. On top of that, her stomach was performing somersaults. And Tyler was wearing an apron and standing at the stove! Billionaires did that kind of thing?

"I wasn't under the impression that we'd be meeting at your place, Mr. Knight," she said grimly.

"This worked out easier for me. I've been running and gunning all day, and the paperwork was here at my place. I'm sorry I had to send my driver over. I'd planned to pick you up myself."

He didn't look at all apologetic.

"You're a very busy man," she told him. "Your driver was very polite, at least."

"That's good to hear. Tony has worked with my family for a lot of years."

Idle chitchat. That's what this was. The thing about it, though, was that she could feel her nerves lessening as she spoke with Tyler. Besides, it was hard to feel nerves when the man was standing there in a silly apron with the motto *Builders Only Use Hard Wood*.

"Do you always wear aprons?" she asked with a semblance of a smile.

"Only when I want to get a real smile."

She tried to wipe the smile away but it grew instead. Damn him!

"It does smell delicious in here. I'm sure you have something planned for later, so we ought to get business out of the way quickly."

The look he gave her made it more than obvious that she was the focus of his menu. Her stomach jumped again.

"My only plans tonight are to begin going over some paperwork," Tyler said before turning back to whatever he had cooking on the stove.

"It would be very helpful if I could study up on the paperwork before we go over it."

"I prefer going over things together. Get used to it."

She sat in silence for several moments, irritated that his personality could so easily turn on a dime, if men like that even knew what a dime was. One moment he was almost pleasant. The next he was acting like a Neanderthal.

Several moments passed and Elena began to grow restless. She wasn't the kind of person who sat around doing nothing. It wasn't in her personality.

"Do you need any help?" She was in no way obligated to offer help, but doing something had to be better than sitting there twiddling her thumbs.

"I'd love help. Want to cut up the salad vegetables? They're all in the produce drawer in the fridge."

Elena got up, moved over to the refrigerator, and, pulling out the veggies, went back to the island. There was no way she was going to stand right beside him as he worked at the stove. She thought about moving back to the sitting side, but that would make it too obvious how much being near him affected her, and that was something she couldn't allow.

Tyler pulled out a cutting board and a ten-inch knife and reached around her to place it on the island, his body brushing against hers as he paused there for a few seconds too long.

"I've got it," she finally whispered, hating the huskiness in her tone.

"Thanks," he replied, and he stroked along her side with one hand before he withdrew.

Elena's fingers were a bit shaky as she began tearing lettuce. It was safer than cutting at the moment. Anything that required expert knife skills wouldn't be wise at this point. She'd get the trembling under control first.

Tyler finished cooking right as she got done putting the salad together, and then she insisted on helping to set out the plates and silverware at his kitchen table. It was at that point that she realized how domestic the scene appeared.

"You realize this isn't a date, right?" she said as the two of them began eating their meal.

Tyler looked up, finished chewing, and then smiled. "What makes you say that?"

"This is work, Mr. Knight." She stressed his name to get the point across. "And I *am* billing you for every minute I'm here. We've been over that subject before."

"We'll see," he said before looking down at his plate and picking up another forkful.

"I want to be very clear. You are being billed for my time. So if you want to waste an hour cooking and eating, you should be aware of that." He needed to get this. She needed to say it to remind herself.

"I'm not worried about it, Elena."

Elena wanted to shake the man. She had no idea what he was thinking, but she knew the way he expected the evening to end — with her in his bed. She would do everything in her power to prevent that from happening.

She barely tasted the food she hadn't wanted in the first place, and she gulped down her wine a little too quickly in her desperation to do something to occupy her hands.

"When would you like to go over the papers?" she said about fifteen minutes into the meal. She just couldn't eat any more of it. Her nerves were fried.

"As soon as we're finished with dinner," he told her, and he was taking his sweet time.

"I don't want to be out too late. I have a case I need to work on tomorrow," she said, hoping he'd respect that.

"What are you working on besides this project with me?"

"It's nothing you'd be interested in," she told him.

"You'd be surprised by what I'm interested in," he said, and he put down his fork.

She thought for a moment about refusing to answer his question, but he obviously was going to keep pushing her, so she settled back with her glass of wine and found herself opening up.

"The work I'm doing tomorrow is pro bono. The case involves a little girl — only five years old. Her stepfather was beating her, and that apparently went on for six months. Her mother worked two jobs and didn't realize what was happening. The girl has been in foster care for almost a year now, and the mom has jumped through a lot of hoops to get her back. She divorced her husband, has taken parenting classes, and has more than proved that she loves her daughter."

"Then will she get the girl back?"

"I think so. It depends on the judge. I hope so. I've only been an attorney for three years, but I volunteered for a children's advocacy agency all through college, and I think I can usually tell when the parents are lying. I honestly don't think this mother is. I hope she gets to reunite permanently with her daughter. Despite all the child has been through, she's such a ray of sunshine. She's a sweet, smart little girl."

"It sounds as if you've gone through a lot of emotional cases," he said, and she was surprised to hear something like sympathy in his tone.

"Yes. But it's been worth it. I think I really do make a difference."

"There are several sides to you, aren't there, Elena?" he said before making sure he had her full attention. "Just like there are a number of sides to me."

His comment derailed what she'd been about to say. Who was this man, really? She knew she couldn't be wrong about him. She knew the old saying about a man being born with a silver spoon in his mouth, and that was Tyler Knight. He was the complete opposite of her.

Sure, he'd lived in a modest home for more than a few years with his guardians, but his inheritance had been sitting there waiting for him to turn eighteen, and when he had, the playboy lifestyle had been on full throttle.

"I've seen one side of you — not the best one — plastered all over the gossip rags," she finally said.

"We all have a story. You didn't bother to find mine out. You just assumed I was an asshole. Do you still think that of me?"

Damn! This man didn't pull his punches. She didn't know how to reply to that question. Should she just be honest with him? Or was this all part of his rich-man games? If only she had a crystal ball.

"I guess I would say yes and no."

Tyler sat there for a moment and then he surprised her when he laughed, true merriment shining from him.

"I enjoy your honesty, Elena. It's refreshing, especially in the world I live in, where everyone besides you is constantly kissing my ass," he said. "Let's move to the living room and finish this."

Without waiting for her assent, he stood up, grabbed a bottle of wine, and began moving. Elena was left with no choice but to follow him. She was almost eager to see what was coming next. How perverse of her, she thought.

CHAPTER TWENTY-TWO

TYLER SETTLED DOWN on the couch and put the bottle of wine on the coffee table in front of him. Where would Elena choose to sit, he wondered? But he knew.

She looked at the couch, and then over at the chair, which was about as far from him as she could get. Predictably, she began heading toward the chair.

"Join me on the couch. We have documents to look over," he told her, and she turned toward him with a look almost akin to fear. "I'm not going to bite, Elena," he said before smiling. "Not unless you want me to."

That comment earned him a contemptuous glare as she walked stiffly toward him and sat so tightly against the arm of the couch that not even a wisp of air could slide between her and the leather. He made her nervous. And he liked that.

"Do you really want to know, Elena, why I asked you to be one of my attorneys?" He scooted closer to her. She gulped from her wineglass. "Maybe you should slow down with that."

"I have a driver — your driver — and I'm an adult," she said, taking another drink.

He could have mentioned that she was also on the clock. He chose not to.

"Yes, you most certainly are an adult," he said instead.

"You were going to tell me why you really hired me," she told him, her eyes wary.

"I think about you day and night. I think about the taste of you, about touching you, teasing you, finally making love ..."

Her eyes dilated. Good. She was more responsive than ever before. But the problem with his words was the way they were affecting his own body. He shifted on the couch as his jeans became far too uncomfortable.

"I haven't been able to work at all lately, and that's not good — I have a lot of important projects underway. But I can't focus on anything but you." Tyler stretched out his hand and rested it on her thigh.

He didn't move his fingers, just let them stay there, let her adjust to his touch. He knew he could take her, knew she would like it. But he wanted her to beg him, to need him. She'd rejected him, and now he wanted her pleading and begging instead.

"Why me?" she finally choked out.

"Why not you?"

"I can't think right now. You're confusing me," she said, setting down her empty wineglass and holding her head in her hands.

"What's wrong?" Was this another act she was putting on?

"I think I drank too much."

Tyler sighed with frustration. He never should have brought the wine to the table. This wasn't how he had planned on his night ending.

"Is that an excuse, Elena, or are you running from me again?"

"I don't have to run from you, Tyler. I can do whatever I want, whenever I want to," she snapped.

"And you want to make love to me."

She held her head back up so she could glare at him. "It must be nice to be so confident."

"Why play modest when I know who I am?"

Her sweet lips opened in an exasperated expression. Tyler wanted to close his around them and end this debate, but he'd never before bedded a woman who wasn't fully accountable for her actions.

"I think I hate you," she finally told him.

"No you don't, Elena. You might wish that you hated me, but you certainly don't."

"I'm ready to go home now, Tyler," she told him through clenched teeth.

"And I'm not ready to let you leave," he said right back.

They scowled at each other for several tense moments and then her expression changed. He couldn't figure out what was going on. She leaned forward and lifted the bottle of wine — their second bottle, and he hadn't had much from the first. She refilled her glass and then sat there and drank it down before looking at him again.

"What are you doing now, Elena?"

"Isn't this what you want, Tyler? You aren't going to leave me alone until you get exactly what you're after, right?" she said. "Me drunk and in your bed. I toyed with the rich playboy, so now I need to put out, of course."

She reached for the bottle again, but this time he stopped her. This game had changed in a way he didn't want it to. Now she was playing the victim. He wasn't such an asshole that he was going to actually use the woman sexually in her condition.

"This is absurd. Knock it off."

"Why? You want me, right? So let's just get it over with," she said as she leaned against him.

"As much as I want you in my bed, I'm not taking advantage of you now."

She turned more quickly than he thought possible in her inebriated state, suddenly straddling his lap and pressing down against the part of him that was throbbing in agony.

Honor. Why in the hell did he have to feel it? This was what both of them wanted — needed. But instead of kissing her as his lower brain told him to, he stood up with her in his arms.

"What's the matter, Tyler? Are you not actually man enough to go for it now that I'm offering it?"

"We can't do this." He could barely speak through the frustration. Was this his fate with this woman?

"Are you not turned on when a woman becomes forward?" she taunted, acting perfectly content to lie against his chest as he held her close to his body.

He grabbed her chin and made sure she was focused on him. "This is not a game," he said slowly before leaning in and kissing her mouth roughly to get his point across. "I want you and I will have you. Just not at this moment. You won't be able to blame alcohol the morning after." Tyler growled as he reminded himself that patience was a virtue.

"Your loss," she slurred.

"You can sleep here tonight. If you still feel the same way in the morning, we'll talk then," he told her as he began walking through his house and quickly made his way up the wide staircase to the second floor. He automatically turned into his own bedroom.

"I don't want to sleep here," she murmured, but her eyes were closing.

"Tough! This conversation isn't finished, but you need to be sober first."

He laid her down and she looked as if she were struggling to open her eyes, but within a minute, she gave up the battle and he groaned again when he realized she had already passed out. Even if he had taken her up on her offer, she wouldn't have lasted long enough for them to make love. And he wasn't the type to resort to the human equivalent of a blow-up doll.

She obviously didn't handle her liquor too well.

After pacing his room for several passes, he moved back over to her and removed her shoes and trousers. The sight of her barely there silky black panties sent a new surge of pain through his body.

She needed water — dehydration was a major threat — and he needed a break from looking at her to try to give himself time to get his libido under control.

He left the room, practically limping from the bulge in his pants. When he returned, she hadn't budged an inch. He woke her long enough to make her drink the glass of water, and then she passed out again.

Sleeping wasn't going to be nearly as easy for him.

Why did he have to torture himself even further? Obviously because he couldn't help it. He lay down on top of the covers — climbing in beneath them with her half-bare body would have proved fatal. When he put his arms around her, she instantly snuggled against him once more.

As he held her against him, he reminded himself that this was just a basic instinct, that she could be any woman. But as his body pulsed, and his heart thudded, he wondered if maybe, just maybe, it was only this woman he wanted.

That certainly couldn't be true. Because if it was, he was surely damned.

CHAPTER TWENTY-THREE

LIGHT WAS CREEPING in through the gap in the curtain when Elena's brain started to reach daytime speed. She was fighting to remember. Where was she? How had the night ended? How had she made it to bed?

Her body stilled. Feeling a foreign weight on her stomach, she looked down and saw Tyler's arm. Then she glanced over, directly into his eyes.

Damn, that was a powerful way to wake up.

"Good morning, Elena."

That was all he said, and yet his words still traveled through her blood and straight to her core. Desire, pure and strong, ran through her. And it was hot and heavy.

"Do you have nothing to say?" he asked, turning them both so they were face to face, his arm around her.

"Where are we?" she croaked.

"In my bed," he replied.

The pulsing of her heart sped up, amazing as it seemed.

"Why am I in your bed?" She didn't so much as move a pinky finger.

"Because you got drunk last night, threw yourself at me, and then passed out." All the while he spoke, he was stroking her back with his hand.

"I see." She wished she could forget the night before, but she couldn't. Everything, every miserable thing, flashed through her mind.

"Have you changed your mind, Elena?" he asked, pushing her tousled hair away from her eyes.

She felt exposed, excited, and unsure of what to do next.

"You won't quit pursuing me until we've had sex; or will you?"

He froze beside her, and his hand stopped running through her hair.

"I'm not a rapist, Elena." The barely leashed fury in his voice told her to proceed with caution, though she wasn't afraid of him. She was afraid of herself.

"I know that," she said. "But you definitely go after what you want."

"Yes, I do. I don't think that's a bad thing," he told her.

"And you've decided you want me, so there's no stopping you." Did she really want him to stop? Lying in his arms didn't feel at all unpleasant. Could she hate him and desire him at the same time? This was something she'd asked herself before. Evidently she could, so it was decided.

"Then I guess we might as well have sex, Tyler."

Only he didn't know it wasn't their first time. She was more than aware of that. Would he remember when he was sunk into her body? She didn't think he would. Would that crush her more than she'd already been crushed? It might.

His movements stopped as he looked into her eyes.

"You'd better make sure this is what you want, Elena. I don't require sacrifices."

He pressed against her, letting her feel his arousal. Heat surged through her, cementing her choice. She didn't know this new Tyler, didn't really know what kind of man he'd turned out to be, but she suddenly knew that if she didn't make love to him again, she would regret it to the end of her days.

He was her first childhood crush, her first best friend. He had failed her in so many ways and she had no doubt that he would fail her again. But why not do what she truly wanted to do?

He'd already taken her once, and it wasn't as if she'd been sleeping around with multiple men. This wouldn't make her a horrible person — just a human. And they didn't make you wear scarlet letters anymore, did they?

"I can admit that I want you, Tyler."

"Are you sure, Elena? I won't be able to stop once we start," he said, his fingers tightening in her hair and his body pressing even closer to hers.

"I'm sure, Tyler."

He reached for her and she held up a hand. "What?" he asked.

"I'll be right back."

She rushed to his bathroom to take care of necessary business. She took exactly five minutes to take a record-breaking shower and brush her teeth with an unused toothbrush that she'd filched from his cabinet.

When she came back out, Tyler pulled her into the bed without hesitation and flipped her onto her back. His eyes were burning with need.

"I thought you might change your mind," he said before bending down and kissing her.

"No. There will be no mind-changing this time," she assured him.

Then he pressed into her and she felt the full weight of his body, his manhood pushing against her heated core. It sent waves of desire up and down her body.

Tyler ran his mouth down her jaw, then her neck. He growled in frustration at the barrier of her shirt as he moved lower, but that problem didn't last long. She basked in the feel of him, and her moans mixed with his. Her fingers trailed down his back as he spread her thighs and rested between them.

He rubbed his arousal against her, and she raised her hips, wanting to skip the foreplay and feel him thrusting inside her. She needed that connection, needed their bodies entwined.

But he began moving, kissing his way down her body, making her quiver with each new place he found, exploring her, feeding her hunger.

When he spread her open and his tongue slowly trailed up her folds, her back arched up from the bed. No, this hadn't been the wrong choice. He was masterful in lifting her toward the greatest pleasure. The feelings were so much stronger than eight years before. Yes, it had been amazing then, but now, now it was indescribable.

Closer and closer she came to an orgasm, but then he stopped, moved to her thighs before drifting back to her little bundle of nerves and circling it with his tongue. She cried out her frustration, but he knew exactly how close to bring her before backing off again, drawing out the agonizing pleasure for what seemed like forever.

When he climbed his way back up her body and sucked on her breast while thrusting his fingers inside her wetness and flicking his thumb across her swollen bud, she tugged on his hair. She was right on the edge now.

Then she reached down, needing to feel his silk-covered hardness. Her fingers found him and she wrapped them around his erection, as far as she could, and squeezed, eliciting a groan from him that she felt through her entire body.

He kissed his way up her neck again. "Are you protected, Elena?" he asked while still pumping his fingers inside her.

"No," she moaned. Did she care? The last thing she wanted was for him to stop.

He turned away from her, and she was actually tempted to yell at him. But he pulled out a condom from a bedside drawer and came back to her.

"Put it on," he said, turning on his side and showing off what he had to give. Impressive.

"Gladly," she told him throatily, grabbing the packet and ripping it open.

She'd never done this before, and she fumbled with the damn thing. And she made him groan again when she was squeezing the tip of his arousal while trying to get the latex on.

"Never mind. I'll do it." Getting those words out was torture.

"I've almost got it," she said with an urgency she knew they were both feeling.

Though it most likely took her five times as long as it would have taken him, he allowed her to finish, and then she ran her hand up and down his hardness a few times.

"I've got to have you now," he said, and he turned her onto her back without delay.

"Yes, now, Tyler!" She wrapped her legs around him and reached behind him to trail her nails along the taut muscles of his back.

She closed her eyes and waited for him, and when it didn't happen immediately, she wiggled.

"Open your eyes, Elena." His words were a quiet command, and she didn't even think of disobeying him.

She looked at him, and then he sank himself fully inside her in one smooth thrust.

She immediately exploded, the pleasure growing more and more intense as her body squeezed around him in hard pulses. He moved slowly, drawing it out as they continued looking into each other's eyes. *So erotic.*

"You are so damn responsive that it takes my breath away," he whispered reverently when she felt the last of her orgasm begin to dim.

"More," she pleaded. She wanted to feel that over and over.

He didn't disappoint her. He began thrusting fast and hard inside her, and her body surged again and again in ecstasy. She'd never be able to leave his bed after this.

When the sun was fully up on the horizon, his body stiffened, and he let go, releasing his own pleasure while buried deep within her.

She grew sleepy beneath him, but the contentment she felt being held in his arms almost frightened her. He rolled over, then pulled her tightly against him.

"You're mine now, Elena."

His words sent both a thrill and terror through her. She knew this wasn't going to have a happy ending for her — their connection was only temporary.

But why not enjoy it while it lasted? She could worry about the fall-out on some other day, couldn't she? At least he wasn't sending her away this time right after he got into her pants.

CHAPTER TWENTY-FOUR

ELENA SAT ON Tyler's back deck and shuddered as a breeze passed by. It wasn't the coldest afternoon in Seattle, yet it certainly couldn't be considered warm, either.

Still, the great view made up for her bit of discomfort. But she had a larger problem. What in hell was she going to say to Tyler now? He'd still been sound asleep when she'd snuck from his bed, taken another shower — a long one, this time — and then found herself wandering outside.

The house was nice, not what she'd been expecting from him. Yes, it was huge, much larger than any single man needed, but there were touches throughout it that made it more inviting, almost … warm. Except out on the deck.

Pictures of him and his brothers along with the older couple they'd lived with as children hung from his walls. Throw blankets rested on the back of a couple of comfortable armchairs in the living room, and the coffee table even had a fishbowl centerpiece. She had to be curious about all that. Had he decorated the place, or had he just paid someone to come in and do it for him?

Most likely it was the latter. That's what little Richie Riches did.

"Is something wrong?"

Tyler's warm breath on her neck startled her. Elena had been so deep in thought she hadn't heard him approach her. After she'd awoken early that morning, they'd indulged in a sex marathon, but it hadn't curbed her desire for this man.

She wasn't sure that a year, or even multiple years, would dull her hunger. At just his nearness, dangerous cravings built up low in her belly.

Agreeing to work with this man had been foolish of her — not that she'd had any choice. Making love to him again had been even more reckless. How in the world could she separate herself from him emotionally if she continued giving him her body?

Oh. He'd asked her a question. "It's just a little cool out here," she told him.

"One minute." He disappeared, but he was back a few moments later with a thick blue throw.

Before she knew what he was doing, he was lifting her into the air, and he sat down, pulling her onto his lap and wrapping the coverlet around her.

She instantly forgot about the cold. It wasn't only the throw that was warming her up.

"Um … thank you," she whispered, wishing she were able to hold herself away, but finding her unruly body curling up against his.

She could tell herself all day that it was for his body heat, but it was just as much for the comfort of being in his arms. This was beyond ridiculous. How could she think of him as her lover now instead of her enemy, and after only a few hours pinned beneath him … and on top of him … and …? She'd always thought she had a logical brain. Still, many people made love while still hating their partners in sin. She apparently wasn't that type of girl. She was unforgivably weak.

"I never sleep past six in the morning, and now it's noon. I feel like a sloth," he said, each word a whisper on the side of her neck.

"I don't think either of us got much sleep, so you have nothing to worry about," she told him. "I do have to go into the office today, though."

"That's true about lack of sleep. I'll gladly go back to bed and spend all day in it — if you stay there with me. Forget about going to work. You work far too much, and what you think you have to do can wait a little while."

As he said this, he unclasped his arms, and slipping a hand beneath the coverlet, he began caressing her stomach. Her instant response was to consider begging him to take her right there and then. Instead, she let out only a small groan when his fingers went beneath her shirt and traveled up over the mound of her breast.

Elena had been feeling so relaxed, but she forced herself to stiffen. She had to get away from this place before she lost her mind. She hadn't had any time to think since they'd made love, over and over, just this morning. It had been so impulsive, and she hadn't given herself a chance to change her mind. She hadn't wanted that chance. But now she had to process what she'd done. And she couldn't do that while Tyler was touching her. Conflict of interest.

"What's the matter?"

His fingers stilled, and when she didn't reply right away, he forced her to face him, with her mouth now only inches from his.

"Nothing's wrong."

"Tell me the truth, Elena."

"I just … this all happened … and now … I just … maybe I should get home and change for work." The words felt as if they were being torn from her throat.

His eyes dilated and his lips compressed, and for a moment she thought he was going to be angry with her. That would be good. If he was pissed off, she could be pissed off, too. But just as quickly as the emotion flashed across his face, it disappeared.

"We make the best decisions when we don't have our guard up," he told her before clasping the back of her neck and pulling her to him. And he captured her lips in a heated kiss.

Elena began losing her battle with herself. Should she just accept what her body wanted so badly?

When she was ready to pull his pants down and hers with them, Tyler released her mouth and leaned back, fire gleaming in his eyes, his lips wet from their kiss, making her want to lean forward and join with them again.

"I could carry you into my bedroom and make love to you over and over again until you don't have a an ounce of fight left," he said, his fingers still on the back of her neck, moving in slow circles that were sending shivers down her spine. "But I'm not going to do that. I don't want you to say that I coerced this. I want you to own it, to love it, to accept that this is where we're supposed to be."

"What does that mean?"

"It means that I'm going to be miserable. I'm going to take you home so you can have time to figure things out. And then, when we come together again, it will be that much better."

There was so much damn heat pooling inside her that the stupid blue throw, which had been wonderful at first, was now suffocating her. Before she thought twice about it, she leaned forward and kissed him, every ounce of hunger she'd been feeling conveyed in her response.

"Okay, we've already made love, so one last time doesn't make me dishonorable," he growled before unzipping her slacks and pushing them and her panties off her hips. "But then I'm taking you home to think."

There was no more talking as Tyler pulled his own trousers down and shifted her so she was sitting on top of him. With a hard thrust, he was inside her, and it was exactly where she wanted him to be.

CHAPTER TWENTY-FIVE

"I'LL BE BY to pick you up in one hour."

"What? Why?"

Elena was groggy as she listened to Tyler's disgustingly alert voice on the other end of the line. What time was it? When she glanced at her clock and saw that it was only seven in the morning, and on a Saturday, she was hardly thrilled.

"I've decided it's time you see my big project. Get up and be ready. I'll bring coffee."

"When did we decide this?" she asked. Elena could never be called a morning person, not on the best of days, but the weekends were her time to sleep until at least nine. Tyler was interrupting that, and she wasn't pleased.

"Right now," he told her. "I have a call coming in, so get up and dressed. I'll see you in an hour."

Elena held the phone to her ear, stupefied. He'd just hung up on her. What she should do is turn off her phone, roll over, and bury her head beneath a pillow. No, those tactics hadn't worked once before. And yes, he was her client, and she needed to make him happy, but she shouldn't have to be at his beck and call, even though they'd made love last Monday.

But then she hadn't heard a single word from him for the rest of the week. What was she supposed to think? Maybe he'd gotten what he wanted and now it was back to business.

Hell! She didn't know. Throwing off her covers, she stomped into the bathroom. It would do her no good to try to go back to sleep now. She was fully awake and irritated as all get-out. She was also wondering how he was going to treat her when he showed up.

After drying off from her shower, she stood in front of her closet stark naked and wondered what she should wear. It was a weekend, and that normally meant shorts or sweats, depending on the weather.

This wasn't an official work meeting, she didn't think, or at least that's what she told herself, so, she compromised by picking out a pair of jeans, a nice cotton shirt, and her favorite sweater.

Then she went over to her dresser and looked in the panty drawer. What if they did end up making love again? She didn't want to be caught with less than sexy underwear. But at the same time, she didn't want to make it so obvious she was hoping for or expecting sex.

Ugh! Dating without actually dating a guy wasn't easy at all. She decided at long last on delicate lace underwear — not because of him, of course, but for her. Decision made, she dragged on her clothes, threw her hair into a ponytail, and brushed on only a light coating of makeup. She was just finishing up when her doorbell rang. Since Piper had been away from home last night, Elena was the only one there.

Still, she wasn't happy with Tyler, and with a little pettiness, she waited until he rang the bell again before she ambled to the door and took her sweet time unlocking it.

The sight of him standing there with flowers in one hand, coffee in the other, his hair hidden beneath a baseball cap, and an old college sweatshirt hugging his chest took her breath away. She didn't have a chance to give him a standard greeting.

He swooped past her, set the flowers and coffee on her table, then came back and lifted her into his arms. His head descended as her lips formed an O of shock and then he was devouring her mouth while his hands gripped her butt and squeezed.

"I've missed you this week. I thought work would never end," he said when he released her lips and set her on the floor.

Elena was slightly dizzy as she tried to get her bearings. That hadn't been what she'd been expecting from him. Not at all.

"You knew where I was," she said, and felt her cheeks flush. She didn't want him to know she'd missed him, or had even noticed that he hadn't called or stopped by.

"I got called to London all this week, and, yes, I know I could have called, but with the time difference and working eighteen-hour days,

I thought it would be better to just come back and ravish you like I've been dreaming of doing."

Maybe he was toying with her. But still, much to her frustration, his words sent an instant glow through her. She didn't want him to get the idea, though, that she was his for the taking whenever he felt like he was getting an itch below the belt. So she repressed that glow.

"What makes you think you have the right to do that?" she said, one hand on her hip as she tried to give him a stern look.

He simply pulled her against him again, knocking the fight right out of her as her breasts tingled and her core heated. He smiled smugly — dammit, the man couldn't miss the effect he was having on her.

"I told you that you were mine, Elena," he murmured against her lips. "And I keep what's mine."

Then he stopped talking, and stopped her from replying as he plundered her mouth again. When his hand slipped beneath her sweater and skimmed up her stomach and over her breast, she sighed into his kiss.

She enjoyed it for a moment, but then she reluctantly pushed away from him.

"Didn't you promise me coffee?" she gasped.

His eyes dilated, and he groaned his disapproval, but he let her go and ushered her to the table where he'd set the flowers and coffee.

"As promised, madam," he said with a bow that had her lips turning up involuntarily.

"Thank you. It *is* the least you can do for waking me up so early on my day off," she told him, trying to sound annoyed but not pulling it off.

Taking a sip of the coffee, she sighed in happiness. A mocha latte — just what the doctor had ordered. She had no idea how he knew her favorite coffee, and she wasn't going to question it. She could totally see him calling her legal secretary and asking, though. No way. That would have been too *thoughtful.*

"I would never have thought of waking you up if I hadn't planned to give you an excellent day," he said with a wink, and he picked up his own cup of coffee.

"And what are we doing?"

"You'll just have to get out of here to find out," he told her.

"Tyler."

"Yes?"

"Thanks for the flowers. They're beautiful." She always had been a fan of daffodils and lilies.

"Not nearly as beautiful as you are," he replied, then gave her his patented megawattage smile. If she weren't careful, that smile could drop her to her knees. She was sure, though, that he would enjoy having her in exactly that place. So convenient …

But even without the smile, the man could drop her to her knees. Her original plan to drop him, even drop-kick him, had been foolish, and everything had turned around on her. But the thing that frightened her the most was that she didn't care — didn't care at all.

"If you are dragging me out, then I insist on you telling me something. What is this big project?" she said, standing firm.

He sighed as if dealing with a small child. She didn't care what he thought about her. Answers were justified here.

"I'm taking you to the Sunriver Children's Camp," Tyler finally said.

"Sunriver Children's Camp?" she asked. She'd heard of the place. It was a hundred-acre plot outside the city, and a massive construction project was going on there. "What do you have to do with that?"

"I'm part of the group building it," he answered.

"How much of a part of it?" she asked.

"It's kind of … well, it's my baby, actually."

"You? Really? This is *your* project?" she asked. This wasn't something she was expecting from a spoiled, pampered playboy.

For just a moment he looked almost hesitant, but soon the look vanished. In its place was his normal confident grin.

"Even assholes do good things once in a while."

She stood there in silence. What could she say to that?

Elena hated this news about Tyler, hated to have something to humanize him with. It was much easier for her to resist the man when she thought of him as an utter bastard. To find that he had a caring side — that was unacceptable, a threat to her sanity.

Then again, didn't really wealthy people look for projects as tax write-offs? That's what this had to be, if only for the sake of her own mental health.

CHAPTER TWENTY-SIX

TYLER WAS ON edge as he drove up to the construction site. Not like him at all, was it?

But this place had been a dream of his for years, and it was in the final stages. Soon, the camp would open, and children with disabilities and who were unfortunate enough to be in the foster-care system would be running through the paths and taking part in the multitude of activities that he and his team had envisioned.

So he didn't quite understand the anxiety he was feeling. All he knew for sure was that he liked this woman next to him. It had killed him not to call her, text her, email her, hell, send a carrier pigeon to her, while he'd been in London.

But he'd told himself he could go a week without talking to her. It had been a little less than a week, actually, but he'd been determined he could do it. That he'd missed her as much as he had wasn't exactly reassuring, but what was he going to do?

Apparently he was going to buy her flowers and pull her into his arms and kiss her until neither one of them could walk straight. But if Elena didn't love the camp as much as he did, he'd be … he didn't know the word he was looking for … was it *hurt*? No way. He couldn't be hurt by that — could he?

Tyler didn't even know this woman, not really, he tried telling himself. But in a short time, she had turned his world upside down more than once, and he liked her, really liked her.

The more he learned about her, the more he found himself thinking that he could spend a lot more time with her. He hadn't thought that possible after the last woman — and her affinity for closets …

"Wow. I've seen the specs of this place, Tyler, but looking at something on paper and actually *seeing* it are two entirely different things," Elena said, breaking him from his reverie.

They were pulling up in front of the main lodge —15,000 square feet and three stories, made of logs, and with giant picture windows and inviting doors. It was certainly impressive, even to a billionaire.

"This is the gathering place for all the campers. I wanted it to be big and beautiful, and more importantly, I wanted it to be inviting. I want this entire experience to be the best of these kids' lives. Some of them won't have anything else like it." He opened the driver's door and came around to her side of the car.

She stepped out and walked with him to the lodge. The doors were open and she could hear the noise of power tools.

"You actually got people to work today?"

"Yes, I have crews going seven days a week. Summer is just around the corner, and I want to be open by July. We have less than a month to go."

"How much more do you have to do before it's completed?"

"We're almost done with construction, so we have to decorate, get the special-needs equipment installed, test it all out, and wait for the final inspection. I've hired only the best of the best, so it's moving along quickly," he told her before officially beginning the grand tour.

They went through the lodge, which had a state-of-the-art kitchen, medical rooms, lounge areas, game areas, and even private nooks with desks for children who would need a few moments to themselves.

"A lot of autistic children have to have quiet time," Tyler said, "and we've tried to anticipate the needs of all the children who will be coming in."

Elena listened to him explain how the rooms were to be used, and how the staffers were being set up. After leaving the lodge, they made their way through a maze of trails with clearly marked signs.

There were several sections to the camp, three-sided cabins taking up a huge portion, and some fully enclosed cabins taking up another section. One area had a cluster of yurts, and another area was more dense with trees and brush and had areas carved out for tents and fire pits.

Each kind of camping experience that you could ever imagine was being put in place. The paths were wide and paved so they were all easily wheelchair accessible, and so were the recreation areas, where the kids could shoot bows and arrows or learn to make a fire, or take part in any number of other camp activities.

When he stopped at one of the enclosed cabins and opened the door, she smiled as she stepped inside. This one had the name "Rockers' Hut" on the outside, and it would be a budding musician's dream come true.

Instruments were painted on the walls, the wooden bunk beds were carved with musical notes, the floor had a drum set etched into it, and the curtains looked as if they were on fire. The closet held a number of real musical instruments, and in the corner a keyboard sat waiting.

"Did you put this much time into every cabin?" she asked as she touched the camp mattress that was just waiting for bedding to be placed on it.

"We aren't finished — not at all — but each enclosed cabin will have a theme to it. The three-sided cabins are all the same, but through the years the kids will personalize those as well."

"So you aren't done with the decorating?" she asked excitedly.

"No, my brothers and I did this one as an example of what we expected. We want each cabin to have its own theme."

"Have you decided on all the themes yet?"

Tyler smiled at the look on her face. "No, not yet. That phase is a couple weeks away still."

"Can I volunteer, please?" Elena asked as she left the cabin and ran to the next one over. He hurried to catch up.

"I'd love that," he said. This woman awed him.

"And I get to do any theme I want? And can I do more than one?"

"Yes. Okay, anything within reason," he said. "We wouldn't want … well, you know …"

"Oh, thank you for sharing this with me, Tyler!" Elena ran back to him and jumped up in his arms, her face shining.

"Thank you for caring," he told her, suddenly choked up with something uncomfortably close to emotion.

He kissed her hard and for a moment she melted against him. But then she wriggled to get down and rushed into the empty cabin in front of them. After scanning the space, she set her purse on one of the built-in desks and rifled through it for a notebook and pen.

"I'm going to do a princess theme in one of the cabins. Yes, the curtains will look like they're made out of satin and lace, and they'll have a gigantic crown at the top. And the walls will be covered with drawings capturing my favorite scenes from the Disney movies — the teapot and rose from *Beauty and the Beast*, for example, and the magic carpet from

Aladdin. Then, we can make dress-up totes for kids of all sizes and maybe even have a salon day at the lodge where the girls can get their hair done. A lot of little girls love to the idea of being princesses." She started scribbling frantically again.

Tyler didn't get a chance to say anything. She filled out a few pages, and then flipped over for the next cabin in line.

"This one will be superheroes. I always thought I was going to marry Superman when I was a little girl, and my first bathing suit was a Wonder Woman one. When I realized later on in life that superheroes weren't real, I was devastated, but everyone, both young and old, still loves a good superhero story."

Tyler leaned against a bed and couldn't help but grinning as more and more ideas kept popping from her imagination. Heck, he might need to build a few more cabins.

He loved each and every one of her ideas.

They spent an hour in the cabin before she finally stopped, then looked at him with a sheepish expression.

"I'm sorry. I've been going on for a while, haven't I?" she said, tucking her notebook back into her purse.

"I could sit here all day and night and listen to you. I love that you want to participate in my vision." Maybe it was time to drag her off to one of the counselors' cabins. Was he changing this much? Maybe.

Just as he pulled her into his arms, the door swung open. With a grumble, Tyler released Elena and turned to find his two brothers in the doorway, stupid grins on their faces.

"Were you planning on christening the place, Tyler?" Blake asked him.

"Sure looked that way to me," Byron added.

"Shut up, both of you," Tyler told them before addressing Elena. "Sorry about my brothers." He could see the heat rising in her cheeks and the way she'd cast her eyes down, apparently in shame. "Don't worry about them. They're full of … words."

"I'm fine, Tyler," she said. "Why don't you spend some time with your brothers while I look at the other cabins. Are they all the same?"

"No, a couple have special bathrooms for kids who have a harder time getting around, and some of the layouts are a bit different," he told her.

"I'll go and look at them while you do whatever it is that you do here."

"I'd rather be with you," Tyler told her.

Blake stepped forward quickly and held out his hand. "We don't want to run you off, Elena. I'm sorry if we embarrassed you. We were just ribbing our little brother."

"Oh, I'm not running off," she said, looking up with a relieved smile.

Tyler realized that his brothers had simply intimidated her. And that Blake had made the gesture to speak to her had effected a world of difference in how she was feeling.

"It's very nice to meet you," Byron said. "Wait. We've met, at the bistro bar, right? Nascosto?"

"Yes," Elena murmured but she couldn't quite meet Byron's eyes.

Tyler was thinking back to that meeting and remembered that Byron had been in a sour mood.

"That's right," Byron said with a smile. He grabbed her and lifted her from her feet, causing a gasp to escape her shocked lips. "I remember that you like hugs," he said before setting her back on the ground.

Should Tyler say something? He hadn't the foggiest. But suddenly her cheeks colored delicately and a real answering smile appeared on her face as she looked Byron in the eyes.

"I do like hugs," she said with a soft laugh.

"Well, then," Blake said before scooping her up and hugging her, too. "It's a pleasure to meet you."

"Why don't you both go hug on your wives?" Tyler groused, and he slipped his arm possessively around Elena's waist.

"Any time, day or night, brother," Blake told him. "Nights are the best …"

"You boys, really, it's okay, go and play. I'm going to look at the other cabins now."

And with that, Elena slipped away.

Tyler turned to his brothers. "Now look what you did. You chased her off."

"She seems capable of taking care of herself," Byron said, and he gave his little brother a pat on the back.

"She's pretty much perfect," Tyler told them.

"That's a big change from what you said a few months ago," Byron retorted.

"Yeah, a lot can happen."

Byron nodded. "I'll agree with that."

Yep, a lot was definitely happening here.

CHAPTER TWENTY-SEVEN

"I DON'T LIKE TO admit when I'm wrong," Elena said as she sat back and enjoyed her s'more. "But I can do it. I'm finding that I might have judged you too harshly for past deeds. We all make mistakes."

"What does that mean?" Tyler asked.

"It's nothing."

"Obviously it's something or you wouldn't have brought it up," he responded.

"Why don't you tell me what made you decide to build this camp?" She really wanted to get the focus off her and her slip in saying too much.

Tyler was quiet as he gazed into the fire, the embers casting shadows on his cheeks, and making it impossible for her to read anything from his eyes.

"I just thought it would be a good project," he finally answered.

"Come on, Tyler. I spoke to one of your managers while you were meeting with your brothers. He said this is a complete nonprofit project, that you've donated all the funds to build it, to get it started, and to ensure that it keeps going. That's not just something a person does on a whim."

Elena shifted in her seat. Tyler wasn't turning out at all to be the person she had thought he was. She wasn't too sure she was happy about that. Had she become too cynical over the years? Was she hoping he was rotten so she was justified in hating him? That didn't say a hell of a lot for her.

"When I was a kid, life wasn't always the easiest," he finally told her.

Elena was taken aback by that response. It certainly hadn't been what she'd expected to hear from him. He'd been wealthy. Sure, when she had met him, he'd lived with his guardians in a smaller home, but later she'd found out who he really was — what he was worth.

Once she'd found that out, she hadn't been surprised that he'd dumped her as a friend. She hadn't been up to his standard of living at all. So to hear him say his life hadn't been easy didn't make sense.

"I have a hard time believing that," she said.

He turned to gaze at her. "Believe what you need to, Elena. I know it's your way of holding yourself back, and I'm not going to convince you I'm somebody other than what you've prejudged me to be, but there's more to a person's character than what first meets the eye."

"Maybe I have made certain judgments, but you have to admit that you have the party-boy reputation going for you," she reminded him. Not to mention that he enjoyed screwing a woman and then tossing her out.

"I worked hard to cultivate that image," he said with a laugh. "In reality, I'm actually pretty dang boring."

She waited for him to add to that. When he didn't she countered him. "I don't think so, Tyler. No one would ever describe you as boring."

"I used to get out a lot more, travel the world, go to places not too many others got to go, had no fear. As my life has progressed, I've had less desire for cheap thrills. Or even expensive thrills."

"That doesn't mean you're boring or that you have one foot in the grave. It means you're growing up and appreciate what you have, and that you don't feel the need to desperately seek out adventure at every turn."

"If you despise me so much, why are you trying to make me feel better about my decisions?"

"I don't exactly despise you ..." She had to trail off. The things she'd said to him so far pretty much meant exactly that.

"You might have before you got to know me, but it's not too easy when you spend time with me. I'm a likable guy." And with that, the cocky smile and his naturally vibrant personality came right back to the surface.

"When you say things like that, Tyler, it doesn't make you too likable."

"Admit it, Elena — you can't live without me."

The problem with his statement was that it could be true. In her short amount of time with this man, he was becoming almost a necessity. But she knew better than to get attached. That would mean certain heartbreak.

But what was she going to do at this point? It wasn't as if she could distance herself from him. He was a huge client for her firm and she was a peon, a mere associate, who had to do what her boss said. Still, knowing that she had no control over the situation made her feel a little better about herself. Sure, she didn't have to sleep with this client — but she'd rather not think too much about that.

"You aren't necessarily bad company," she conceded after an absurdly long silence.

Tyler laughed before moving from where he was and picking her up, then sitting down with her straddling his lap.

"Let's see if I can get an upgrade to great company," he told her.

Before Elena was able to reply, he kissed her, knocking all thoughts from her brain except for how much she wanted him. His lips caressed hers, and she voluntarily opened to him, the warmth of the fire on her back, the heat from his body engulfing her.

"I can't get enough of you, Elena. Even after I have you — several times — I want you again. Tell me it's the same for you." His voice was thick and rough.

As he spoke, his hips surged upward, his jean-clad arousal pushing into her, making her curse the clothes between them.

"Tell me, Elena," he commanded her before gently biting down on her bottom lip and sliding a hand up the front of her shirt. He cupped her breast, and she moaned.

She wriggled against him with abandon. Why should she care anymore that he knew the power he held over her while she was locked in his arms?

"I want you, Tyler," she gasped. "I want you all the time."

Her reward was a renewed assault on her lips while he squeezed her nipple through her bra and rolled it between his forefinger and his thumb. This time their lovemaking was different. She felt a desperation in his touch, in his possession of her. She felt as if he were claiming her — heart, body and soul. And she loved it.

He trailed his hand down her back, then moved it between them. He unclasped her jeans and slid inside. She pushed against his fingers as they found her moist center and began moving in steady circles around the part of her pulsing with the greatest need.

She didn't care that they were outside, in the open. She didn't care about anything but what she was feeling. Satisfaction was coming; he was building it with his brilliant strokes. While his fingers worked their magic, he continued caressing her mouth with his lips, and she moaned into them.

As she reached her peak, Elena bit down on his bottom lip to keep from screaming out, and she shook in his arms. When the initial waves of pleasure had passed, she pulled back and looked into his burning eyes.

"Your turn," she whispered, enjoying the jolt of hunger she saw in him when she said those words.

She began to slip off his lap when a noise stopped her. Tyler heard it at the same time, and he locked his hands around her back.

The sound grew clearer — footsteps approaching, coming closer and closer.

"Busy, bro?"

Elena was mortified when she heard the sound of Blake's voice.

"I thought you were leaving an hour ago," Tyler growled.

"Got held up at the lodge. We were just coming out to say goodbye," Byron piped in. "We aren't interrupting anything, are we?"

He knew very well he was interrupting — his mocking tone of voice made that more than clear. Elena was only grateful that her clothes were in place. They wouldn't be able to see her undone jeans or her hard nipples, which were pressing against Tyler's chest.

"No, not interrupting," Elena squeaked right before Tyler countered that.

"Yes, you are. Go away."

"No prob."

Blake and Byron just turned and left. Elena was blushing like wildfire, and she couldn't even turn to look at the two men as they retreated. After a few moments she struggled to break free from Tyler's grasp.

"We're not finishing, are we?"

"I can't believe I did that out here. I have no earthly idea what I was thinking."

He finally let her go. She jumped to her feet and straightened her clothes.

"That you can't think clearly around me is a good thing, Elena. Most people aren't lucky enough to have this much passion between them." Tyler also stood up and began pursuing her.

She kept backing away. "I'm a lawyer, for goodness' sake, Tyler. I can't act this way."

"Last time I checked, you were human too. Enjoy the thrill. Enjoy letting go."

She bumped into something and realized it was the wall of a cabin.

Tyler moved right up to her and boxed her in against the wall. "I am living a full life," she panted, unable to focus with him so close.

"Prove it," he told her with that wicked smile.

Elena knew she should turn and walk away, knew Tyler threatened her very sanity. But he was right. There was a thrill of doing the unexpected, of being on this constant high.

Without another word, she dropped to her knees on the ground in front of him and with shaking fingers undid his jeans. Her desire outweighed her fear of getting caught with her pants down — or, more accurately with Tyler's pants down.

By the time they were done, she was very satisfied. She had most certainly proved that she could bring him just as much pleasure as he brought her, and that was a thrill she hadn't even known she had wanted to feel.

CHAPTER TWENTY-EIGHT

ELENA WAS DELIGHTED that it was now June. And the market was full of great things.

She shopped every outdoor market she could find when the weather turned. Even if she didn't really need anything.

"Okay, this took some major digging, so you know that you owe me big-time, right?" Piper said as they walked between vendors.

"I know it's almost not worth the information," Elena told her. "You're going to draw this out for as long as you can just for your own sick enjoyment."

"I'm hurt — no, I'm devastated — that you would think such a thing," Piper said, the smile on her face as big as the one on the Cheshire cat.

"Just spit it out, Piper. Seriously, it's been a long week, and I'm worn out."

"Maybe that's from all that sex you've been sneaking in," Piper told her. "The sex that you think you're being so darn discreet with."

Elena stopped what she was doing and turned toward her friend in shock. "How in the world do you know?"

"Oh, come on, Elena. A woman doesn't glow the way you're glowing unless she's getting sex. And not just any sex, but the sort of sex that rocks your body for days to come. And I'm not using the word *come* lightly. I'd almost kill to get that in my life right now," Piper said with a melodramatic sigh.

"Okay, fine, I've had sex with Tyler, and, yes, it's good sex …" Why hadn't she told her best friend about the situation?

"And you're waiting for my judgment, right?" Piper asked.

"Yeah. I was complaining about him for weeks and then all of a sudden I'm doing it in every position known to man. Well, maybe not *every* position … I was embarrassed to tell you about it," Elena had to admit.

"You know that I would never judge you, never be anything but here for you," Piper told her friend. "So don't hold out on me again."

"Fine. I won't hold out on you. But now you can tell me all this mysterious information that you've discovered."

"As much as I do enjoy holding out, this is too good not to share. It appears as if your apparently fantastic lover," Piper said with a long-suffering sigh before continuing, "is also quite the humanitarian. It's a bit disgusting, if you ask me."

"I don't follow," Elena said. "What does that mean?"

"It means that he has served in Third World countries, taking medicine and food to the needy. And then he has multiple projects going on here in Seattle, such as donating funds and even working — we're talking hammers, nails, and more. Sweat equity. He builds houses, volunteers at shelters, and even coaches a baseball team made up of disadvantaged kids."

"What do you mean disadvantaged kids?" Elena asked.

"All of this info and that's what you focus on?" Piper said.

"One thing at a time," Elena told her.

"He has a baseball team of kids from ages eight to ten that are from the foster-care system."

Elena didn't know how to process this information. How could she continue hating a man who volunteered far more than she did, and who seemed to love the same causes she did? Especially when that man was also one hell of a lover?

"How did you find this out?"

"I told you it took a lot of digging. But I managed to get chummy with his secretary last night at the bar," Piper said. "Yes, I did stalk her a bit. If this guy is seeing my best friend, I want to know more about him. But I did that because I was able to do some research through an old friend who works for human services. Tyler doesn't allow his name to be used in the media for his good deeds, and to keep him out of it is no small task, but I think the guy honestly does this stuff because he loves to do it. It's clearly not a publicity stunt, and not just a tax write-off. This man might actually be a decent guy."

"I don't understand any of this, Piper. You know about that one-night stand with him when I was twenty. And I watched him for years in the media. He was always sporting a new woman on his arm, attending the best of the best parties, getting openly drunk and making a fool of himself. We're in split-personality territory here, and how is that possible?"

"I don't know, darling. I just know what I've found out. And this guy is pretty much a girl's dream come to life, if you ask me."

"It doesn't really matter though, does it?" Elena said.

"Why would you say that? He obviously worships you, and he's pretty much perfect. I would think you'd be elated right now."

"There's a big difference between worshipping someone and enjoying sex with them, Piper. Yes, we're having great sex, but that doesn't change the fact that we barely know each other, and that there's no way this will end with me in a wedding gown. I'm enjoying him, but it's only until this job with his contracts is done."

"How do you know that?" Piper asked. "Maybe this is the man you're supposed to be with for the rest of your life. If you don't give it a real shot, you might always wonder about what you could have done differently."

"And if I let myself believe that this is something more than it really is, I'm going to be devastated when everything goes down in flames. Hell, when I crash and burn yet again."

"Don't do that. You haven't had the best of luck with men. But maybe you haven't, because Tyler is the one you were supposed to wait for. If you had settled with some guy that makes you kind of happy instead of ecstatic, you would never know what real passion and real love feels like."

"I think you've been reading way too many of your library books — from the romance section, of all places," Elena told Piper. "Real love doesn't exist, sweetie. Good sex can happen, companionship can happen, but I'll say it again — *real love doesn't exist*. I've seen far more examples of bad relationships than good. Divorce rates are higher than ever before, and if you look around you, even right here on this street, everyone will have a story of a failed romance. I think what you're looking for is a myth. We can enjoy each other for a while, but we eventually grow bored, or we discover that we really don't have anything in common after all. Or maybe the eyes begin to stray. Sure, it's amazing in the beginning because the hormones are running rampant, but in the end, our imperfections come to the surface and epic romance we felt in the beginning is all over in a flash."

"You're depressing the hell out of me, Elena. I refuse to believe that real love doesn't exist."

"I don't have to try to prove it to you, darling. You'll see it for yourself when I'm sitting at home eating ice cream because I miss this man. I have no doubt that when it ends, I'm going to get hurt. I'm just trying to prevent total devastation."

"I'll bet you a hundred bucks that you're wrong," Piper said.

"Would you be serious for five seconds?" Elena sighed.

"I'm deadly serious. On your wedding day to this man, you will hand me a hundred-dollar bill," Piper told her.

Elena smiled. "And when he dumps me as soon as he grows bored, you'll be handing one to me. At least then I can go get a pedicure and soak my sorrows away."

Piper grabbed her hand and shook it. "It's official. Now, no more lying to me. I want all the sordid details," Piper said. "Especially the size of his biggest tool."

Elena found herself blushing, blushing hard, though she really didn't know why. Of course she was going to tell Piper everything. It's what friends did.

"You're definitely right. I need to tell you all. It will be good for me. But for now let's stop talking about any men."

Piper agreed and they strolled through the market. Elena had started a game that Tyler had quickly overtaken her at. She could be depressed about it, or she could just agree that at least she was on one hell of a good ride for the time being.

CHAPTER TWENTY-NINE

*B*E READY AT *midnight.*

That was the text message Tyler had sent to her phone, and for several hours Elena kept changing her mind on whether she was going to be ready or not. She wrote back to ask what they were going to be doing so late.

No response.

Just that short message and then nothing. When it hit eleven thirty and she found herself dressed and pacing the small apartment, she knew she couldn't fool herself any longer. She was going because she had to go. She had to see what this was about, had to know what Tyler had planned.

His driver picked her up right as the clock struck midnight and Elena said nothing; she just followed him to the car and climbed inside. They took maybe half an hour's drive and then the car stopped at what appeared to be a private flower garden.

She knew that questioning the driver would do her no good, so she waited as he held open her door and smiled at her.

"Right this way, ma'am."

Turning she moved to the path and was surprised when she saw that it was marked by lanterns every few feet. The darkness still surrounded her, still made the trek slightly spooky, but Elena knew nothing bad could happen.

Curiosity kept her moving forward.

Even knowing she was safe, she looked at shadows and her heart thudded as she continued to walk along. Why did this have to be at midnight and what was the secrecy all about?

"Elena."

His voice was a whisper in the wind, and she stopped at the end of the trail when she finally saw Tyler, another shadow among the trees.

"Tyler, what's going on?"

"I'm glad you came." He stepped up to her, and her heart began beating at high speed for an entirely different reason now.

"I was too intrigued not to," she told him. "But I did think about ignoring your summons."

"You want excitement in your life, Elena. It's why we connected at the bar, and it's why we're together now. I just want to give that to you."

"I don't need excitement. I'm perfectly content with my life the way it is," she countered, though a voice inside her told her otherwise. She'd been merely surviving before she'd met Tyler for the third time.

Since being with him, she felt as if she were truly living — even if that life was dangerous.

"Come here."

Tugging her into his arms, he latched his mouth on to hers with such possession that she had not a single moment to think of anything other than responding in kind.

One hand rested on the back of her neck, tilting her face up to him, while the other gripped her hip and drew her closer. With a moan of pleasure she melted against him, enjoying the thrill of feeling his hardness press into her.

When he released her, it was a moment before she could speak, and she wished there were more light around them. Then she might have been able to look into his eyes. But she was also enjoying the intimacy of their surroundings.

"You did all of this for a booty call?" she finally said.

"That's dessert," he replied with a laugh. He released her only to take her hand and lead her around a corner to a lawn where a large blanket was laid out with lanterns, wine, fruit, cheese and crackers, and what looked like some good chocolates sitting on it.

"This is a lot of effort to get me into bed, Tyler."

"I already have you in my bed, Elena. This is because I find that I like romance again."

Holding her hand while she sat, he then joined her and poured them each a glass of wine. The burst of alcohol was exactly what she needed at that moment. She didn't know why, but nerves were fluttering through her.

"Just when I think I've gotten you figured out, you change up the rules and do something like this," she said.

"We never figure anyone out fully."

She thought about that for a moment. "What happens when I no longer intrigue you, Tyler?"

"I don't see that happening anytime soon."

He hadn't said it would never happen. She hadn't missed that. But she didn't want to think about it right now. Looking at this man in the soft lighting he had around them, she decided she had wasted enough of her life being cautious.

She was the one to initiate the kiss this time.

The stars shone above them, peeking through the overhanging trees. The evening air had a coolness in it, but with the heat the two of them generated, she didn't expect to feel it at all.

Tyler stroked her neck with work-roughened fingers before he began undoing the buttons of her top. And then his lips trailed down the path he was opening up.

Every touch of his scorched her, and just as she'd known, the night air didn't have the slightest effect on her. But his mouth certainly did. With a quick flick of his fingers he undid the front clasp of her bra, and then was caressing her hardened peak with the warmth of his tongue. He groaned around her nipple, the vibration adding to the sensations coursing through her.

"Tyler," she sighed as she dug her fingers into his hair and pulled him even closer.

"The feel of you beneath my lips makes me lose control," he said before moving to the other breast and giving it equal attention. "The taste of you, the smell of you, the feel. It's all perfection."

He moved lower, his lips skimming along her stomach as his fingers began undoing the buttons on her trousers. She lifted her hips to make it easier for him to discard them and her lacy undies.

Knowing they were outside in a park added to her excitement. It was decadent, and thrilling, and she wanted him even more than the first time she'd lain beneath him. Yes, she doubted she'd lose her law license for public — and pubic — indecency; he must have secured the place from any intruders.

She grasped his hair. "Take me, Tyler. Take me right now."

He fanned his breath over her already hot womanhood. She loved the feel of his tongue caressing her folds, but she wanted more than that right now. She wanted him sinking within her. Nothing else would do.

Feeling her urgency, Tyler climbed back up her body, quickly discarded his own clothes, and settled between her thighs.

"I can't get enough of you," he whispered before slowly, sinking sweetly inside her.

"More, Tyler. I want more." And she bucked up against him, trying to urge him on.

He smiled, his features barely visible as he pulled back and then slowly sank within her again.

She wiggled beneath him, pressure building ever higher as he refused to quicken his movements, just continued to move slowly in and out of her as he caressed the side of her face with gentle fingers.

"So beautiful," he sighed. He leaned forward and kissed her so tenderly that it brought tears to her eyes.

No. This was wrong. This was too intimate, too personal. This was so much more than sex — it was making love, and it was … perfect.

"Tyler, please," she begged.

"Let go, Elena," he told her. "Give me all of yourself." He moved a little faster, but he was still caressing her lips with his own and then trailing his mouth down the side of her neck. All the while he was running his fingers through her hair, along her jaw, and down her side.

The pleasure growing within her was unlike anything she'd ever felt before. It was so much more intense, so much stronger. She felt him in every fiber of her being.

"Let go, Elena," he said again as he thrust into her up to the hilt, pressing his body all along hers, filling her completely with his hardness.

And Elena did let go. She shattered completely, beyond anything she knew. Yes, there was pleasure, more pleasure than she thought possible, but her heart burst at the same time with love for this man — love so powerful that she knew she couldn't fool herself any longer.

As he groaned against her throat, finding his own pleasure deep inside her, she wrapped her arms around his back and clung tightly to him. She didn't want him to see her face, didn't want him to see what she was feeling.

When their breathing slowed to something approaching normal, she tried pulling herself together, but they were still connected intimately.

"Ah, Elena, that was exquisite," he said.

"Yes, Tyler, it was," she whispered.

He tried to raise himself up, but she clung tightly. "Not yet. Tyler. Just lie here for a moment longer."

"I've got to be crushing you."

"No. You're keeping me warm."

Elena was unsure how long they lay there together, but the heat from their lovemaking eventually drifted away and the chill of the night gave them no choice but to drag their clothes back on. They finished their wine, ate the snacks, and then she held his hand as they headed back to the car.

"What about all the stuff we're leaving behind?" she asked when he climbed inside the car with her.

"I have people coming right now to pick it up."

They sat together in silence as his driver drove them to Tyler's house. Elena thought about requesting that she be taken home, but her lover would question her too closely if she did that. And though she knew she was in love with this man, she couldn't tell him that, couldn't give him her secret.

So she accepted what he was giving her, and hoped it would be enough. It had to be enough.

CHAPTER THIRTY

"LET'S GO, NOLAN. You've got this!"

Elena sat back and watched as Tyler coached his Little League baseball team in practice. It hadn't been hard to find out where he was when she'd called his oldest brother, Blake. The man had sold his little brother out in an instant.

Why hadn't Tyler shared this with her yet? Insecurity filled her at the thought. Of course, there was insecurity in all aspects of her relationship with Tyler. Even though he was good to her, almost too good to her, that scared her.

It was too good to be true.

And this was obviously something important to him. So here she was, hiding in the corner as she watched him coach these young kids.

He was good at it, very good.

The boy hit the ball and went flying around the bases. Tyler was out in left field smiling as Nolan made a home run.

"All right, kids, last batter," Tyler called out.

Elena watched in confusion as the young boy to his left began creeping up behind him. What was happening here? Then the kid got a silly grin on his face as he tugged on a loose string hanging down from Tyler's shirt.

At that moment, the batter connected with the ball and the kids were running for it while the batter tore out, base by base, toward home. Tyler looked at the boy who had found such amusement in pulling on the string, and he ruffled the boy's head. Then they all began dashing back to the dugout.

That's when Tyler's eyes connected with hers.

Letting his assistant coach begin packing up the equipment, Tyler jogged over to her.

"What was that about in the field?" she asked, embarrassed at having been caught. "I mean with you and that little boy."

"That's Albert," Tyler replied. "He's been fascinated with the string on the bottom of my shirt all day."

"You really seem to enjoy coaching these kids," she told him.

He was quiet for a minute, looking as if he wanted to say something, then one of the children came running up to them with a gigantic smile.

"Coach Knight, I got my report card today," the boy said, holding out the piece of paper and waving it.

"How did you do?" Tyler asked, kneeling down.

"Only one B. All the rest are As," the boy burbled.

"Nice job, Bobby." Tyler high-fived the kid. Then the rest of the team members were also pulling out their report cards. After a chaotic few minutes, Tyler bestowed a brilliant smile on the members of his team.

"All of you are not only passing but also on the honor roll. Do you know what this means?" he asked.

"Yes!" everyone on the team shouted.

"Pizza time," Tyler told them, and the kids began rushing toward the two vans waiting in the parking lot.

"Pizza time?" Elena asked.

Tyler looked a little uncomfortable when he answered. "They get a reward for doing well in school."

"I think you've really changed through the years haven't you, Tyler?"

He looked puzzled for a moment, and Elena bit her tongue. She didn't want to reveal her humiliation of that night to him. Finally, he spoke. "You made assumptions about me. Lots of people make those assumptions, but everyone does change as they grow up. We have to be a little bad for a while so that we know how to be good." Then he winked and moved in closer, his words quiet so no one else could hear. "However, if it's an asshole you want, then I can be that too."

"Oh, I know you can be that, Tyler. But I didn't say that's what I wanted."

"Sometimes I don't know what you're expecting from me."

"I don't either. But you're no longer a spring chicken, unlike the children you coach, so I guess I should cut you some slack. Midlife crises can be the worst, I'm told."

"Coach, coach, we're waiting for you," one of the boys said, coming up and tugging on his shirt.

"We're heading out, Leo. Load up on the bus." The kid followed the rest of the team and then Elena was alone with Tyler.

"Would you like to join us?" he said.

So the guy had some balls, and the offer was tempting. But Elena decided that she'd been overloaded enough for one day. Maybe next time she would go. But if she kept doing these sorts of activities with him, she would believe they were in a real relationship. And that might well endanger her mental health.

"I need to work on some notes at home. You go enjoy your team," she said, turning to leave.

He grabbed her arm and stopped her movement. Elena looked up at him warily.

"Why are you here, Elena?"

"I wanted to see you coach," she told him.

"Why?" he asked.

"What do you mean?"

"What made you want to see me coach?" he asked.

"I'm just trying to figure you out."

"Have you yet?"

There was a long moment of silence, too long, since he really did need to get going.

"No," she told him.

"Maybe you should try harder."

"And maybe you should do the same favor for me. How hard have you been trying … other than in bed?"

"I'd be trying *hard* now if I could." With that, he turned and walked away from her.

Elena moved to her car and waited a while to start it. Tears were suddenly pressing against her eyes. There was no doubt she was in love with this guy. Maybe if she stopped fighting that feeling, she could find a hint of happiness with him, even if it only lasted a few days, weeks or months.

Wasn't it better to have loved and lost than never to have loved at all?

CHAPTER THIRTY-ONE

WALKING THROUGH THE same garden where she'd made love to Tyler the month before, Elena wondered why she would want to torture herself by returning to this place.

"You've been quiet for an awfully long time," Piper told her.

"I know. I'm trying to gather my thoughts, trying to figure out how to tell you what I need to tell you. Nothing's easy anymore."

"You know you can tell me anything, Elena. That's what best friends are for. We're supposed to talk to each other, share, and be there with a shoulder to lean on. Yeah, okay, that's all trite crap from self-help books, and I'm ashamed that I even said it. But what do you expect from a librarian?"

"I've messed up, really messed up."

"Okay, Elena, you have to tell me what in the world is going on," Piper said insistently.

"I'm pregnant."

Elena's words were followed by a long silence. The two of them stopped on the trail they'd been walking down.

"How far along?" Piper asked.

"Probably about a month. I think this is the place I actually got pregnant," Elena said with a sad sigh.

"You got pregnant in a public park?" Piper said, sounding just the slightest bit jealous.

"It was spectacular sex, but as with all good things, there are consequences."

"Do you want to keep the child?" Piper asked.

"There's no question about that. I've been scared, but I already feel a connection with the life growing inside me."

"Have you told Tyler?"

Of course her friend didn't bother to ask who the father was. Neither of them was the kind of women to have any doubt about parentage. They didn't screw around.

"No, I haven't said anything yet. I don't know how to tell him."

"But you will tell him, won't you?"

"Yes. He has a right to know," Elena said. "But I'm worried. We've never talked about feelings. Yes, he makes these over-the top statements. I belong to him, and he desires me. Serious, no? That's the extent of it. We can't raise a child together just because our sex life is spectacular."

"No. You can't get married because of a child. You might have a few months or even a few years together where everything is okay, but if you aren't in love, then eventually you'll grow to hate him, and he'll hate you. That's not good for either you or the child."

"I do love him," Elena said quietly.

"I know you do," Piper said, while placing her arm around her. "Does he love you?"

"I don't think so. I know he wants me. I know he appreciates me. And I even know he's not the monster I once thought he was. But I don't think love factors into his basic set of emotions."

"He loves his brothers, doesn't he?" Piper asked.

"Yes, I believe he does," Elena told her.

"Then we know he's capable of love. Maybe you should just come out with it and tell him that you love him."

"I can't do that," The very thought of it made Elena's heart race.

"Would you rather always wonder what could have been," Piper said, "or would you rather dive in with both feet forward?"

"I think we've already dived in with both feet. I'm carrying his child," Elena told her.

"Yeah, that's true. But anyone can make a baby together. To spend a lifetime with another human being takes a special kind of magic. You have to tell him how you feel or you know you'll always regret holding back. You need to know how he feels about you before you tell him about the baby or you'll also always wonder."

"When did you get so dang smart?" Elena asked her friend.

"I read a lot," Piper told her with a laugh.

"I guess that's an occupational hazard."

Joking with her friend helped lift Elena's spirits, but only marginally.

She had to tell Tyler the truth, had to share with him that they'd created a child. But she was still terrified.

"Why don't we spoil ourselves at the day spa, then have a wonderful dinner and make some baby plans. If you focus on the miracle you have growing inside of you, you can't possibly be stressed," Piper said as she switched directions and dragged her best friend along with her.

"I haven't had a lot of time to focus on the 'miracle' of being pregnant," Elena told her as her hand trailed to her flat stomach. "I'm going to be a mom."

Terror and warmth both filled her at the thought.

"And I'm going to be an honorary aunt. It's certainly a day to celebrate."

"I'm glad I told you," Elena said as they reached their car.

"I'd be crushed if you hadn't told me."

Elena didn't know how she was going to talk to Tyler, but at least she'd never be alone, not with her best friend right there by her side.

CHAPTER THIRTY-TWO

"**Y**OU'VE BEEN UNUSUALLY quiet this evening."

Elena sat across from Tyler in his living room and smiled, though it took a lot of effort to do. "I just don't feel all that well," she told him.

"In fact, you've been quiet all week," he said. "Why?"

"I just have a lot on my mind right now. It's no big deal."

"I've discovered its best to let you speak when you're ready. I'll let you tell me about it when you're ready."

Several long moments passed where only the sound of the antique clock ticking could be heard. Drawing her knees up, she clutched her legs to her chest, a protective gesture. She'd been in this room several times, but as she looked around it now, she felt as if she didn't really belong here.

Her eyes focused on a picture and she vaguely remembered the couple with three young boys in front of them.

"Did you love your guardians?" she asked.

Tyler looked over to the picture that had drawn her attention. He seemed to be thinking over what he wanted to say.

"They were very good to us," he finally told her.

"So you didn't love them? You just appreciated that they took good care of you?"

"No. I wouldn't say that. If I had to pinpoint it, I think they taught me what love really was. They loved each other so much that when Vivian died a few years ago, Bill was devastated. It made me wonder if I would ever want to put myself through that."

"Put yourself through what?" She was so fascinated with what he'd just said that she loosened her grip on her legs.

"Through the pain of loving and losing someone."

"Without risk, Tyler, there's no real life to be led."

"There are different levels of risk, Elena. I think it's one of the reasons I sought adventure for so long. I enjoyed all that risk, all that excitement. Kind of like watching horror flicks. But after a while, I found that even seeking thrills became boring."

"Then what exactly are you looking for?"

"Why all these questions, Elena?"

"I'm just trying to understand you a little more," she told him. "What made you believe that your guardians were so in love?"

He was thoughtful for a moment as he gazed at the picture of what looked to her like a perfect family. Three smiling boys with a couple most would assume to be their grandparents.

A truly loving family had been everything she'd always wanted.

Yes, she knew how hard it had been for the young boys, and how hard it still must be for them with their tragic family history. But that picture still left her with a sense of longing in her heart. At least the brothers had had people to replace their lost parents, whereas her father had left when she was very young, and no other family was around to fill the gap. If she thought she might get that fulfillment from Tyler she was very wrong. But for some reason she was still looking for it in him.

"I guess it was the way he touched her. There was no thought to it — just instinct and true affection. He was simply driven to seek her out no matter where they were. He could be talking to someone, to anyone, but he just knew the moment she approached. He would move slightly, his hand fluttering to her side, his leg brushing hers. It was subtle and it was intimate."

"You noticed this at such a young age?" she asked with surprise. "That sounds pretty romantic for a young boy."

"It was Blake who pointed it out. But I was pretty observant even that long ago. I just liked to watch people and how they interacted. I don't know why."

"Do you still like to do that? Watch people, I mean."

"Yes. I still try to figure out people's stories. Everyone has one, you know."

"Yes, I agree with that. I am quickly learning in life and in my career that everything isn't always as it seems. There's so much beneath the layers of protection that people build around themselves."

"What layers do you have protecting you, Elena?"

This made her pause. Should she be completely honest with this man? He sometimes appeared to be opening up to her. Okay, she'd try.

"I don't want to be hurt. I've had my ups and downs in life like everyone else. I have abandonment issues — excuse the psychobabble — as most children do who lose a parent at an early age. And I've never fallen in love before, though it's something I want. It would be wonderful to have someone touch me without thinking, to need me so much"

"And what about living in the moment?" he asked her.

"I think living in the moment is good as well. 'Seize the day,' and all that. But then I think there's a time when we have to grow up and strive to find what really makes us happiest in the long run."

"Are you happy now, Elena?"

"What do you mean by that?"

"I mean, do I make you happy?" Tyler asked her.

This was a loaded question, and again she wondered if she should tell him everything. Knowing that she was carrying his baby and not knowing how he would feel about that made her afraid to reveal too much. She needed to know whether he cared about her before she could tell him about the child. She would tell him — there was no question — but she'd like to know how he felt about her first.

"I care about you, Tyler." Her heart raced as she told him that.

"I feel the same way about you," he said with almost a real smile.

"Why are you still unmarried? Do you prefer brief relationships?"

He was silent for several moments as if really thinking about what he wanted to say next. They'd talked about sex, about chemistry, about living in the moment. But they hadn't discussed something as loaded as a future. It wasn't who they were.

"Sometimes I'm almost addicted to being alone. Long-term relationships make that impossible," he finally said.

"What's the longest relationship you've been in?"

"Last year I thought seriously about asking a woman to marry me. That was until I found her in the broom closet with another man at my brother's wedding."

That shocked Elena. It hadn't been what she'd expected to hear. "You don't seem too upset about that, Tyler."

"I was upset for a while. I didn't have a mental breakdown or anything, but it made me a little wary of the opposite sex. It made me prefer being alone."

"One person screws you over, so everyone who looks like her must be bad? Is that your opinion?"

"Once burned, twice shy. What can I say? Then the next woman I pursued ended up playing games with me." His eyes connected with hers as he made this statement.

"And you didn't play any with her?"

"Turnabout is fair play, Elena."

"It's always easy to judge when you're in the driver's seat," she said before going for the gut and the gusto. "And how did that relationship end up?"

He set down the drink he'd been holding and moved over to where she sat. "I don't know. I'm still trying to figure that out," he told her before grasping her hands.

Maybe it was the dimly lit room, maybe it was the way he was looking at her, and maybe it was just because she was in love with this man, but as he cupped her cheek and looked deep in her eyes, Elena let go of her fears.

He leaned forward and pushed her back on the couch, stretching his body over hers, moving slowly, more intimately than usual. It nearly brought her to tears.

He bent forward and traced the seam of her lips with his tongue. A sigh opened her mouth to him, inviting him inside. She felt her core quickly warming to him.

He tasted dark and rich, sweet and spicy. He explored her mouth, his touch both seductive and dark, as if he was barely keeping a leash on his hunger. She writhed beneath him. As he took ownership of her, she knew that she might not have his love, but she certainly had his attention.

But for how long?

She would tell him about the baby tomorrow. She needed tonight to be about only the two of them.

CHAPTER THIRTY-THREE

WALKING IN A bit of a daze, Elena wasn't sure what to think. Yes, she'd already known she was pregnant, not only because of the stick that had shown her a plus signal, but because she could feel the small changes in her body — the nausea, tender breasts, and abnormal need for chocolate.

But to be walking from the room in the hospital where they had confirmed her pregnancy, she found herself in deep thought. This was real. There were no more excuses not to tell Tyler the truth.

Still as the shock began to dim, a tender smile lit her face. There was a baby she would be responsible for in seven and a half months, a baby who would hopefully have Tyler's eyes and determination, and her smile and love.

Turning in the hallway as she headed for the exit, she wasn't paying attention to where she was going, and she ran smack dab into what felt like a brick wall. Before she was able to catch herself, she flew backward, and she felt a sharp pain shoot through her ankle when she landed on the floor.

Tears instantly sprung to her eyes as her hand instinctively cradled her flat stomach. "My baby," she gasped, ignoring the pain in her foot.

"Your baby?"

Elena froze as her head slowly tilted. She knew that voice. This wasn't how she'd been planning on telling him. She had wanted to go to his house, sit down, and talk. Her eyes drifted along the solid thighs and hard chest of Tyler who was looking at her in total shock.

"I didn't see you there," she gasped before looking around. No one else was anywhere near them. "Why are you here?"

"I was going to ask you the same thing," he said before his eyes shifted, zeroing in on her hand, which was still cradling her stomach.

She quickly shifted to try to get up, but pain sliced through her ankle again. Dammit! She didn't have time for an injury right now.

"I asked you first," she said, deciding she rather liked where she was sitting.

"You said the word *baby*," he practically snarled.

Elena decided that silence was probably in her best interest right now. This was neither the time nor the place to have this discussion. Certainly not while her brain seemed to be scattered and her foot was throbbing.

"Can you stand, Elena?" he asked, finally taking his gaze from her stomach to where she was testing out her ankle.

When he kneeled down and ran his large hands along her tender ankle, she couldn't prevent the squeak of pain that escaped her.

"Obviously not. You've hurt your ankle," he answered his own question.

"I'm fine. Just go away and let me get my bearings back," she said. Not that she thought those words would do her any good. He didn't appear to be going anywhere.

Before he could say anything a nurse came around the corner and spotted them.

"Is everything all right?" the man asked.

"No. Ms. Truman has hurt her ankle. Can you get a wheelchair?" Tyler said before she was able to tell the man she was fine.

"It's not that bad," Elena said, but the nurse was already turning to go and do Tyler's bidding. The man seemed to have that kind of effect on people.

"You're obviously not fine, Elena. We will get your foot looked at and then you will tell me what you meant about a baby," Tyler demanded.

The nurse was back in a flash, and then before Elena could protest further, Tyler was lifting her from the ground and depositing her in the contraption. He walked next to her while the nurse pushed her straight back to an examining room just like the one she'd recently vacated.

Tyler was silent as the nurse disappeared, assuring them the doctor would be right with them. Elena refused to look at him. If she pretended he wasn't there, maybe the man would just disappear, giving her time to think.

That didn't happen.

A knock sounded on the door, and the same doctor who'd examined her about fifteen minutes ago walked in. She held her breath, hoping he wasn't going to say something that was going to make this situation worse.

"Ms. Truman, the nurse said you had a fall in the hallway," Dr. Ortega said, taking a seat in front of her.

"Yes, I'm sure it's nothing, but my ankle is a little tender," she told him.

He felt her ankle, making her cringe. "It feels like a sprain, but we'll send you in for an X-ray to make sure. I'm going to also do an ultrasound to make sure the baby wasn't hurt. They are pretty protected inside you, but it's better to be safe than sorry."

Her luck just wasn't with her.

"Yes, an ultrasound would be good," Tyler said.

There was no inflection in his voice to give her any clue at all to what he was thinking. And she was too scared to look at him to try to read the expression in his eyes.

"Are you the father?" the doctor asked.

"No," Tyler said. "We just ran into each other in the hallway."

Elena's heart shattered at his words. He was acting as if they were complete strangers.

"I'm sorry about that. We're going to examine her in here, so if you want to wait outside," Dr. Ortega told him.

Elena still didn't look at Tyler. If she did, she was surely going to fall apart.

"I'll be outside," Tyler said.

She didn't look up until she heard the door closing in the most final-sounding click she'd ever heard. Why would he bother waiting? He didn't think the baby was his, and he'd obviously just decided their relationship was over.

"Lie back and we'll get started."

Time stopped having any meaning at all while Elena's stomach and ankle were checked. Her foot would heal fine, the doctor said. They wrapped it, and she was able to move slowly despite the minor sprain. But the fall — at least that's what the doctor thought — had caused her blood pressure to spike to dangerously high levels, so he decided he wanted to keep her in the hospital overnight.

She tried to argue with him, but when he brought up the safety of her baby, she gave in. As much as she wanted to go home and curl up with some ice cream and a lot of tears, she wasn't about to put her baby's life in danger.

The upside of being admitted was that it took a while to get her moved to her room. She was hoping against all hope that Tyler would grow impatient and leave. That would give her more time to pull herself together. Because their next words to each other weren't going to be pleasant.

CHAPTER THIRTY-FOUR

TYLER PACED THROUGH the sitting area in that part of the hospital as he tried to figure out what in the world was going on. When he'd called Piper to find out where Elena was and she'd told him Elena was at the clinic at the hospital, he'd panicked, and had immediately gone searching for her.

What had happened was not what he'd been expecting.

She was pregnant. That thought stumbled around inside his mind. Was it his child? He didn't take her as a cheater, but still … He was always careful, always used protection.

Except for one night.

They'd used nothing at the park.

But if she were pregnant, why hadn't she answered him in the hospital corridor? The only explanation he could come up with was that she knew it wasn't his child, knew that a DNA test would prove that. Otherwise, wouldn't she have told him the moment she knew about it, wouldn't she be trying to get him to marry her and get a nice healthy sum of money for herself?

That was the only thing that made sense to him.

So he should be thanking his lucky stars. This should end his obsession with this woman. He was too hooked on her, too infatuated. Since she was pregnant, that meant she hadn't been faithful to him.

But with whom? And when had she had the time? None of that really mattered, though, did it? A baby changed everything. It was over between them. But why was he still pacing in the waiting room like an expectant father? Why hadn't he left yet?

Because Elena still held power over him. Maybe he wanted to hear it from her lips that the child she carried wasn't his. That had to be what it was.

So when too much time passed and he discovered she was being admitted to the hospital overnight, he tried to tell himself it wasn't worry that he was feeling; it was simply a case of loose ends.

He waited longer.

Picking up his phone a few times, he almost dialed his brothers. Almost asked for their advice. But he didn't want them to know about this, didn't want them to see what this woman had done to him. They already knew that he'd been obsessed with her ever since he first met her in that bar.

To add this as icing on the cake was unacceptable — they'd never let him forget it.

Nothing lasted forever. Hadn't he learned that at a young age? His parents had been worthless, had screwed up his brothers for years. He'd only escaped that fate because he'd been too young to understand at the time what was happening.

Yes, Bill and Vivian had stepped in and offered a great example to the three boys of what good people were about, but one couple didn't change what a person saw all around them.

Dammit! If only a Magic 8 Ball really worked and he could just find one, shake it, and have all the answers he needed. Hell, with his luck, he'd probably get "Better not tell you now."

Finally, Elena had a room number. He immediately sought her out.

"Are you okay?" He stopped at the side of her bed.

"I'm fine. You should have left. There was no reason for you to wait for over an hour."

"You ran into me in the hallway, and you were hurt, Elena. I wasn't leaving." His voice was filled with exasperation.

"You're not helping my blood pressure by snapping at me," she said, and she couldn't help but look daggers at him.

"Are you going to tell me about this baby?"

Her skin tone grew even more pale, though he hadn't thought that to be possible. He almost wanted to take the words back. She was obviously injured, or the physician wouldn't have checked her in for an overnight stay. Maybe he should have given her some space.

"I was going to tell you about the baby tonight, Tyler. I've known a couple weeks but it wasn't yet confirmed."

"What exactly were you planning to tell me tonight?"

He couldn't seem to back off. There were so many emotions running through him, and rage was the one closest to the surface. Why had she ruined this thing, whatever it was, that they'd had between them?

She looked away from him, and that rage somehow managed to intensify. How in the hell could he read her expression if she wouldn't even make eye contact? She seemed to do that a lot — maybe it was something she'd been taught in law school.

Showing a gentleness he didn't think possible at that moment, he placed his hand beneath her chin and raised her face so she had no choice but to look at him.

"I'm owed an explanation, Elena."

"I don't owe you anything, Tyler," she said, a hitch in her voice.

"So did you go straight from lying beneath me, from screaming out my name, to fucking another man?"

That question made her eyes blaze with anger. She thrust his hand away from her.

"You're disgusting, Tyler. I want you out of this room," she snarled. The monitors at the side of her bed began beeping. "And I want you out of my life."

He leaned down on the bed, his own temper high. He waited until he knew he had her full attention.

"I will get answers, Elena. Don't doubt it for a second. I'm neither weak nor pathetic, and I don't like anyone making a fool out of me."

"Sir, you need to get out of the way. I have to check on this patient."

A very irritated nurse moved to his side and pushed him back. He could have easily resisted, but Tyler wasn't in the mood to fight with the hospital staff.

"I'll be back." Great. He was using dialogue from *The Terminator*.

With that, he stormed out of the room. He really needed a strong drink. Or three.

CHAPTER THIRTY-FIVE

CRYING HERSELF TO sleep hadn't been a good idea, because when morning came, she woke up to a marching band in her head, and it was breaking every noise regulation in Seattle. Pain radiated off her in waves, and she couldn't prevent the whimper from escaping.

There was no way she was opening her eyes. She felt around for the call button to the nurse. Medicine. She needed painkillers *stat*.

"What do you need, Elena?"

Her pain ratcheted up another notch at the sound of Tyler's voice. He was the reason her head was pounding and her ankle throbbing. So his voice was definitely not the first thing she wanted to hear this morning.

Until yesterday, she'd quite enjoyed waking up to his resonant voice.

She really wished she'd called Piper. If she had, her friend would have stayed by her side all night and not let Tyler into her room. She would have attacked if he'd tried to get past her. That's what best friends did.

"Does your head ache?"

"Yes," she murmured.

"I'll shut the blinds so it won't hurt you to open your eyes."

His footsteps seemed to slam against the floor as he moved to the window, and the squeaking of the blinds as he drew them together made her head pound even more. Then he was back at her bedside.

The nurse came in, bringing her pills before disappearing again.

Tyler remained surprisingly quiet. After about fifteen minutes, the pounding hadn't disappeared, but it had lessened enough that she could finally open her eyes.

But she wasn't sure she wanted to take that radical step.

"You were restless as you slept. Normally, you don't move a muscle, but for the past couple of hours, you've been tossing a lot."

"What are you doing here, Tyler?" she croaked out. "Nothing has changed from last night."

She pushed the buttons on her bed, raised it to a sitting position, and reached for the water glass that was on her hospital table.

"I told you I'd be back so we could talk," he replied.

She waited for him to add something to that, but he just sat there next to her bed, his expression showing her nothing. Why in the world was she expecting anything different?

Tyler Knight was still the boy who'd abandoned her as a child and then taken her virginity and walked away when she was twenty. She'd been nothing more than property to him, and now he had a perfect excuse to break ties with her. She wasn't going to be such a sex goddess while sporting a big baby bump.

With a sigh of frustration she threw off her covers and slowly edged herself out of the bed. It took several moments, and though her ankle hurt, she managed to stand.

"What are you doing?"

"Using the facilities," she said, before staggering slowly into the bathroom and firmly shutting the door.

Her first glimpse in the mirror made her wince. She looked like hell in a handbasket. Her hair was a mess, with pieces sticking out in every direction, probably from her running her fingers through it five thousand times, and her face was colorless and sickly. Damn. She'd been hoping when their relationship ended that she would at least look great.

Ugh!

When she came out of the bathroom, Tyler was right there, offering his arm. "I've got this," she told him, terrified of feeling his fingers on her right now. She needed to stay strong.

If he touched her, that wasn't going to be possible.

Her progress was slow. And once she managed to climb back into bed, a nurse came in with her breakfast and checked her vitals. Elena didn't mind the interruption.

"The doctor will be making rounds in the next hour, but your blood pressure has gone down significantly. I don't see a problem with him releasing you today." The woman breezed back out.

"Elena, it's time we talk."

"Fine. What exactly do you need to know?" she asked, pushing aside her breakfast. Nothing looked appetizing at the moment.

"I think you know the answer to that," he said quietly.

"You know I'm pregnant, Tyler. So do you want me to say it out loud? Yes, the child is yours, though I'm insulted that I'd even have to tell you that."

He studied her the way a child with a magnifying glass might look at an insect.

"I don't believe you."

Elena stared at him in complete shock. After a few heartbreaking moments, she composed her features and waited to reply until she was sure her voice would come out clear.

"Why don't you believe me, Tyler?"

He paused as he gave her another once-over. "I think it's a ploy to gain a wealthy husband."

Elena fought tears. How in the world could she have fallen in love with this pitiful excuse of a man?

"Why don't you tell me exactly how you feel?" she said, and she didn't try to hide her sarcasm.

"I'm just calling it as I see it. Do you have any better explanation for what's going on?"

"No. I don't. I guess you figured me out, Tyler."

She turned away, unable to look at the man she'd given her heart to.

"Dammit, Elena. I'm trying to understand. If you gave me even a small reason to trust you, then maybe …" He trailed off.

She might as well tell him it all now. What did it matter anymore?

But it wasn't easy to speak, because she had a lump in her throat the size of a softball. "You used to be my best friend, Tyler. Years ago."

He'd been about to say something, but her remark stopped him in his tracks. He gazed at her with mistrusting eyes and waited for her to say more.

She stayed silent; she wanted her words to have time to truly sink in.

"Explain now!"

"Do you think that yelling at me or trying to intimidate me is the way to get me to talk, Tyler? Seriously!"

"I'm frustrated. Just tell me how we knew each other."

"You called me Lanie. You dumped me when I was ten because I didn't apparently kiss you the way a real girl does." Wow, so much bitterness. Maybe she wouldn't be feeling it now if it weren't for the rigid way he was standing there, or the hostility shooting from his eyes.

"Lanie?" he finally said, his brow wrinkled as he thought back to his childhood.

When he repeated her nickname, it tortured her, and a few tears slipped from her eyes.

"I think I've made a mistake," she choked out. "You aren't that boy I once knew, and I'm not Lanie anymore. That little girl faded away a long time ago."

He was silent for a while longer, and then the look he sent her made chills travel down her spine. He seemed to despise her at that moment, and she didn't think there was any possible way for her heart to break any further than it had.

"You sought revenge on me for something I did as a stupid child?"

"I was drinking, and it just happened," she said.

"That's your only excuse?"

"That wasn't the only time you hurt me, you know. You did it again when I was twenty years old."

"Come on, now. I didn't see you again until we met in that bar," he roared.

"That's not true!" she yelled. Then she stopped and took a calming breath. "It doesn't matter, Tyler. It was a long time ago. I'm sorry. Would you just leave now?"

This wasn't getting either of them anywhere.

He looked at her thoughtfully for a moment. "Did you know that when I was a teen I tried to find you, but you no longer lived in that house, and because it was a rental, I couldn't even find out what your last name was. Then I went through a period of my life where I was selfish and didn't think of anyone. By that time, our friendship was gone."

"You searched for me?"

"Yes. My best childhood memories are from the time we ran around together, playing until nightfall, and laughing for hours on end. I knew that I had hurt you. But I was an adolescent boy. An idiot. For you to blame me for almost twenty years for that is just wrong."

"Are you telling me that you don't hold any grudges, Tyler? You always forgive and forget? I don't think so."

"Well …"

She broke in again when she got her voice back. "It wasn't just that," she said. "I saw you again when I was twenty."

His expression still showed her nothing. So she didn't know what he was thinking about when he asked her, "And what did I do?"

"I was working at a gentleman's club as a waitress. I was still a bit gangly, and very unsure of myself. You were there with a group of men who were less than gentlemanly, and you … you made me feel about two inches tall."

"There's no way …," he insisted.

"You lured me into your limo and fed me a couple of drinks. We had sex that night, Tyler. It was the first time for me. And you immediately walked away."

Silence greeted that statement. He didn't show her what he was thinking. She was holding her breath as she waited for even a moment of recognition.

"I would remember that …" He wasn't sounding as sure now.

"Then maybe I'm making the entire thing up so I can guilt you into giving me fifty percent of everything you have."

She said these words so coldly in hopes that she'd make him walk away. She couldn't do this anymore, couldn't even stand to look at the man, let alone talk to him. Every insecurity she'd ever had was rising to the surface, and it was painful. So very painful.

"Yeah, maybe you are," he said before looking at the exit like it was an open door to the nearest chocolate factory. "If you have anything else to say, now would be the time."

"I guess I do have something to say," she told him, smiling as sweetly as possible. "Go straight to hell and never come back."

He looked at the floor and then at the ceiling, but didn't look at her again. And then he was once again walking out on her. She was used to seeing his back, so she didn't know why it was breaking her heart into a million pieces now.

No. That wasn't true. She knew exactly what was happening. It was what she'd known would happen from the moment she'd decided to have sex with him. He was leaving with part of her as his souvenir.

She closed her eyes and counted to a hundred, cutting off the final tears she was going to allow herself over Tyler Knight. She knew he'd end up with her heart — he'd always had it. She was actually amazed that he'd left her with anything, especially with his child.

CHAPTER THIRTY-SIX

TYLER GAZED OUT his office window and sighed in frustration. It had been a month since he'd walked away from that hospital room, a month since he'd seen Elena. He told himself he was better off, that she was a liar, that she had played him.

So why in the world did he feel like hell? Why did he hurt every time her name flitted through his mind? It didn't matter how many times or in how many ways he told himself that she'd fooled him; he still felt that same ache.

Standing up so quickly that his chair went flying across the room, he glared into the sunny blue Seattle skyline. Even the weather was mocking him. He wanted clouds and gloom, and instead the world went on its merry way, indifferent to his pain.

People sailed on the water, his camp had opened and children frolicked and laughed there. His brothers reveled in their lives with their lovely wives, and in showing off their children — they were all pictures of perfect domesticity, damn them. The Earth kept spinning in its usual way, according to the laws of physics, while Tyler felt that he was spiraling out of control. Okay, he was subject to gravity, but not that kind of gravity. He felt weighed down, depressed, *grave*. The night of the living dead or something.

Would she now get married, settle down, and have a dozen kids and star in a reality TV show? Was this everything she'd ever wanted? To find a weak man whom she could use, but who wasn't her true companion?

That wasn't who Elena was. She was his, dammit!

But he'd walked away.

Tyler dug his fingers through his hair and rubbed his chest, where a permanent ache seemed to be lodged. This was ridiculous. He should have forgotten all about this woman by now.

But what if the child was his?

Sagging against the window, he put his hands out and the ache only grew bigger. What if the child wasn't his? Did he even care? Was he willing to raise a child that wasn't his?

Of course he cared. He'd been cheated on before. It was what women did. His mother sure as hell hadn't known how to stay faithful, and it had cost her and his father their life.

But his sisters-in-law would never cheat. How did he know that? Just by looking at them. It didn't matter what had come in their lives before they met his brothers. They were in love, happy, and devoted.

Wasn't that what Tyler had always wanted? He didn't even know anymore. Before he had a clue what he was doing, he was in his car and heading down the road. As he flew across the city, he watched the sun set. Of course it was beautiful, lighting the sky with purples and oranges. The very beauty of nature was even mocking his misery.

After pulling up to Elena's apartment building, he sat in the car and looked up at her door. What was he doing there? What did he plan to say to her?

She certainly wouldn't welcome him inside. Not after the last words they'd exchanged, the mistrust between them. He should call off this mission and drive away. It's what was best for both of them.

Instead, he found himself opening his car door and then he was walking, moving toward her stairs, and then he was standing in front of her door. Whether he was ready for this or not, it was coming, because his fist lifted almost of its own accord, and he knocked loudly.

The door opened and he saw the surprise on Elena's face. He could see she was trying to decide whether or not to slam the door shut. A myriad of emotions fluttered across her face, and he watched her mask it into polite boredom. It was the worst expression she could give him.

As if he meant nothing at all.

His eyes drifted from her face to her stomach. It was still flat, but inside it grew a child. Was it his? Again, did he care?

"Hello, Tyler. What are you doing here?" Her voice held no emotion; it was level and lawyerly.

"Invite me in, Elena." Did he look almost maniacal? Probably, and he was definitely acting that way. He was holding his hand against the door in a gesture that assured her he wasn't going in any direction but forward, like a door-to-door salesman of old.

"Now isn't a good time. I'm working on a case file and ..." She didn't bother saying more. They both knew she was simply making an excuse. Why expand on it?

He moved forward and she took a step backward. If it were fear on her face, he would have been horrified. But it wasn't fear, not of him anyway. He had no doubt of that. She couldn't ultimately hide her reaction to him.

She was afraid of his touch, afraid of what that would do to her. Well, he was afraid too. Because he couldn't seem to live without this woman.

"Tsk, tsk, Elena. It's incredibly rude to leave someone standing in your doorway." And with that he brushed past her, walking inside her place. "Where's Piper?" He didn't stop until he made it to her living room.

He heard the front door shut and then her footsteps as she practically stomped after him.

Damn, he'd missed her. He'd missed her laughter, her fight and her drive, her smell, the way she tasted. He'd missed each moment of each day he'd spent with her. Tyler didn't care what had happened between them, didn't care that each of them had hurt the other. All he cared about was that he wanted her in his arms — and he didn't want to let her go ever again.

"It's also incredibly rude to barge into someone's house, Tyler. You weren't invited, and I have a lot of work to get done," she told him, her cheeks flushed in her anger.

"Yes, I was brought up badly, Elena — you know my history. So it goes. What have you been doing this past month?"

She looked at him as if he had two heads. Maybe he did. He'd certainly made enough wrong choices in life to blame a split personality on, at the very least. Multiple personalities.

"What are you doing, Tyler? Why are you here?"

"I've missed you. I want to know what you've been up to. Isn't that what people ask when they haven't seen each other for a while?"

Her mouth gaped open. "You need to leave, Tyler. I can't ... can't do this," she said, and much to his horror he saw tears appear in her eyes.

Just as quickly as they'd appeared, though, she blinked and then she was shooting fire at him. The tears gave him hope. The fire made him glad. She wasn't a weak woman. She couldn't be broken. And damned if he hadn't tried.

What a fool he'd been.

"Are you expecting someone else to stop by?" he asked, trying to sound casual.

"What in the world are you talking about?" she replied.

"Are you with anyone, Elena?"

"With someone? How?"

"Do you have a man in your life?" It almost choked him to even say the words.

Her mouth dropped open again, and then her eyes blazed with far more heat and outrage than he'd ever seen before. She was the personification of the phrase "seeing red."

"Yes, Tyler. Of course I'm expecting a guy to drop by. Any minute now, too. So I would really like you to leave. I have to rush off to the kitchen, shed all my clothes, drape my body in nothing but Saran Wrap, and open the door to my lover. He'll peel the plastic off. Slowly? Quickly? Who knows? Who cares? We'll get it on right against the freaking door."

That image filled Tyler with rage. It made him shake, and he had to calm himself before speaking again.

"I can't stand the thought of you with anyone else, Elena." Sheesh. How could he admit such a thing? Was he another weak man, just like his feckless father, who'd been duped so disastrously by his mother?

She looked at him, confusion dominating her face.

"Are you ... jealous?" she sputtered.

"No, of course not!" he snapped as he rose and stepped closer to her. Then he calmed down. "Maybe," he added, reaching for her.

She stepped back and he followed until she had nowhere else to go.

"Don't touch me, Tyler."

He could see her panic. "Why not, Elena?" He leaned closer, but didn't actually touch her.

"I can't handle it, Tyler. Please, you have to leave me alone."

"I've messed up, Elena. I can't go a single day without thinking about you. The thought of any other man coming near you makes me go insane. We both played games, but it can't be too late for us. In the beginning of all this, I admit that all I wanted was a good time in bed, but then it changed. I didn't even know that it was changing. Yes, I don't give my trust easily — I've told you some of the reasons — but I've realized while you've been gone that I need to let those go. My life is only half full without you in it. Forgive me. Please."

He didn't touch her, didn't move back, just waited for her to respond in any way.

"What about the baby?" she asked.

"It really doesn't matter to me. If she's your child, then I will love her."

He meant that. He would love the child for no other reason than because he loved her. And anything that was a part of her he would cherish.

"I don't understand this change." She had every reason not to trust him right now. He'd been far from trustworthy.

"She's mine, though."

"Wait. What?"

"I'd decided on the drive here that I didn't even care if she was another man's, that I didn't care what you'd done during our relationship, because I wanted you that much. But now I know that you wouldn't have been with anyone else. You aren't that way. This is my child."

"Is that what this truly is about, Tyler? You've figured out this child is yours and you don't want to miss out on raising him or her?"

"No, Elena. What this is about is that I love you. And because I've realized how much I love you, I know this child is mine. But even if she, or he, weren't, I would still love you. If we'd just met today, I would fall in love with you. Because you're my other half, and fate has brought us together many times in our lives. Why else would we keep finding each other?"

"Do you remember the gentleman's club?" she asked.

"Yes. After you said what you said at the hospital, I did some soul searching. I ran through my mind of all the shitty things I've done in my life. I remember a waitress, I remember your face and I remember my friend being a dick, and the way I laughed. I did that because I wanted him to leave you alone. I didn't defend you because I was an asshole. That group was a bad group. That was my last night out with them, if it makes any difference."

"What about the limo?"

He didn't want to admit to this. It showed who he had been then, and it wasn't a good man.

"I was drunk for a year straight back then. I did some horrible things. But yes, I remember. I tried to black that time out in my life. I didn't know you were a virgin. I didn't even see you back then. But now I know and I hope you forgive me."

He waited for her verdict, afraid of what she would say next. He seemed to be afraid of everything right now. But most of all, he was afraid of losing her. If he could gain her love again, he knew everything else would work out.

"You're in love with me?" she finally whispered.

"Yes, Elena, so in love with you." He leaned forward and gently kissed the corner of her mouth, then skimmed his lips across hers, his touch soft. "I love you so much I hurt," he added as he pulled her close.

And he nearly jumped for joy when she melted against him.

Picking her up, he moved to the couch and cradled her in his arms.

"I thought I was happier alone, that if I didn't give you my heart, there was no way to get hurt again. But it wasn't my choice whether to give it to you or not. It's always been yours, I think, even from the time we were kids. I just had to grow up enough to realize that."

"I should slow this down, tell you that we've been moving too fast this whole time," she murmured against his neck. "But I can't find it in me to deny you. I've also missed you so much. I also hurt without you." Her tears warmed his skin.

"I'm so sorry I've hurt you," he told her as he caressed her back.

"Don't do it again, Tyler."

"I swear I won't," he said before moving away — just a little — and holding her face so she could see into his eyes. "We'll marry and you can teach me every day how to be a better man."

"That's your idea of a decent proposal?"

"What's wrong with it?" he asked.

"What makes you think that a nice girl like me would marry a man like you?"

"Should I have added the words *If you'll have me*?

Elena laughed before leaning forward and kissing him, this time long and slow. When she broke away they were both breathing heavily.

"That's a start. I will marry you, Tyler, because you have so much to learn."

He carried her into the bedroom, and he wasn't sure who was teaching whom by the end of the night.

EPILOGUE

"DON'T SPEAK TO him, don't make eye contact, and don't leave the car."

Piper Covington stood there listening to the security man, who was wearing an earpiece, and she had to bite her tongue.

Who in the hell was this client she'd given up her Friday night to drive around? She had no idea. Some ultrawealthy asshole with more money than brains, she was sure. Her brother owed her big-time for this. If he didn't get new drivers — and soon — he was going to be up a creek without a paddle, because she was done dealing with men like the one she was giving up her weekend for. She'd already worked more than her forty hours at the university library, dammit, and she was tired as sin.

"You need to acknowledge me, Ms. Covington. Now."

"Got it, chief." This came through gritted teeth.

"If you have an attitude, this isn't going to work," he told her.

"I'm not going to change my personality. But I do know how to follow rules. If your boss leaves me alone, I can certainly leave him alone."

"What is going on here?"

A shudder traveled down Piper's spine at the deep baritone voice right behind her, sounding far from pleased.

"I'm sorry, sir. I wasn't expecting you out so soon," said the wretched man who had been chewing on her hide for the last fifteen minutes.

Ignoring his employee, the man stepped in front of her, and her first look at him left her speechless. That wasn't something easy to do — she loved to talk. After all, she spent her life with books, with millions and millions of words.

Towering over her, with dark hair and nearly black eyes, the man before her didn't look pleased. His chiseled jaw was locked tightly together, his firm lips in a frown. She didn't bother looking down at the rest of his body. She could guess what she'd see. Just his head was a cliché from romance novels, though her library didn't have many of that sort, at least from after the nineteenth century.

That was until she remembered she wasn't supposed to make eye contact. She ripped her gaze away and stared at his chest. It was covered by a tailored shirt that hid nothing. Hard. The man was hard. Hard-bodied, that was. And probably hard in almost every other way. *No, not that way ...*

"Who are you?"

"Piper Covington. I'm filling in as your driver this evening," she said.

"What happened to Jared?"

"He got a stomach flu."

"Hmm."

She didn't know if that word, or, more accurately, that sound, was good or bad. So she said nothing.

"We'd best get going then, shouldn't we, Ms. Covington. It's going to be a long night ..."

New erotic romance spin-off series coming up for preorder soon!

Continue Reading for an Excerpt from:

HER UNEXPECTED HERO

By
Melody Anne

Published By
Pocket Books

PROLOGUE

"HELP . . ." A GURGLING cry whispered faintly on the wind, and three teenagers walking by turned and listened.

"Did you hear that?" Spence asked.

"I think so. It sounded like someone yelling, but I'm not sure," Camden replied.

"Please h-help . . ." This time there was no mistaking the cry. It was faint, but the three boys turned toward the lake.

"Someone's in trouble," Jackson said, and he took off sprinting in the direction of the sound. Spence and Camden were in hot pursuit behind him. They ran the short distance to the shore and spotted a body thrashing around in the water. As they neared the water's edge, they saw the kid's head disappear below the surface.

The three teenage boys stripped down to their underwear in seconds, then dived into the freezing water without hesitation. All of them strong swimmers, they quickly reached the part of the lake where they'd seen the boy and plunged beneath the surface, frantically searching for him.

Spence was the first to reappear from the deep water, the boy in his arms. Camden and Jackson flanked him on either side and the three of them towed the boy to shore. Jackson pulled the wet clothes from him, then grabbed his own clothing and used it to cover the boy, hoping it would bring him some warmth.

Meanwhile, Spence began mouth-to-mouth resuscitation, with Camden doing chest compressions. The three of them worked relentlessly, and after what seemed like hours, but in reality was only a couple of minutes, the boy began coughing. Spence quickly turned him on his side as water spewed from his mouth.

After struggling for several moments to cough up the remaining fluid in his lungs, he looked at his three rescuers with large green eyes. His confusion quickly abated, and he remembered what had happened and how close he'd come to losing his life.

"Y-you . . . s-saved me," he gasped, then started choking again. Spence patted him gently on the back. The kid couldn't have been more than ten or eleven years old.

"What were you doing in the water?" Camden asked as he glanced back out at the lake. He was looking for a boat or something.

"I w-was s-skipping . . . rocks on th-the . . . d-dock and s-slipped." His teeth were chattering so hard that Spence, Camden, and Jackson worried he'd break them. The three teens were also starting to shake as their adrenaline subsided and their wet bodies began to feel the chill in the air.

"Michael! Michael! Where are you?" a man was heard calling out only seconds before he walked over the small hill with several people trailing behind him. He spotted the four boys and came running toward them. "Michael, what happened? Are you okay?" The man dropped to his knees.

The people standing around him looked at the boy, whose clothing was half off, and then at the three nearly naked teenagers.

"What is going on here?" one man demanded, sending the teenagers a suspicious glare.

Before Spence could say anything, another person stepped in. "Aren't you three living in the Taters' house?"

Camden hung his head in shame. They despised living in the filthy foster home, but because they were together, they didn't complain. Each of them had been tossed from home to home practically since birth. During their two years together at this latest home, they had developed a bond rarely found in such circumstances.

It made the bad food, threadbare clothes, and their housemother's screaming fits all worth it. The three of them could face the world as long as they had each other. But if they complained, they would get separated and probably never see each other again.

"Yes, sir, in the Taters' house," Spence replied through chattering teeth as he tried to puff up his chest. As the oldest, he had to protect Camden and Jackson, even if that meant that he took all the heat upon himself.

"What are you doing with Michael?" another man asked, and his tone implied it certainly couldn't be anything good.

"They saved me," Michael said. His eyes gleamed with hero worship as he looked over at the trio.

"What happened, Michael?" the boy's father, Martin, asked as he embraced his son.

"I was skipping rocks and fell. I couldn't stay above the water. They pulled me out." Michael's eyes shone with unshed tears.

Martin looked from his son to the three boys, who were beginning to turn blue, and then at the crowd gathered around. The men's expressions changed from suspicion to awe in a few heartbeats.

"You're heroes," one man said as the rest of the group murmured their surprise and agreement. Spence, Camden, and Jackson looked at each other before Spence spoke to the crowd.

"No we're not. We were just the first people here," he said with a shrug. Although relieved they weren't suspected of foul play, they still weren't good enough to be called heroes—at least not in their minds.

The men rushed into action: someone made a phone call, another person draped warm jackets over the boys' shoulders, while still another gathered their discarded clothes and handed them over. The normally unseen boys stared wide-eyed as everyone moved around in a blur, all the attention focused on them. None of them knew what to do or think. This was completely new for all of them.

They watched as an ambulance arrived and pulled up to the edge of the grass, then all four of them were carefully led to the vehicle. Spence, Camden, and Jackson were in such shock that they weren't able to speak—no one had ever worried about them before, and they couldn't quite process what was happening. So they sat in silence while the paramedics examined them.

They were taken to the emergency room, and then transferred to a private room in the back, where medical staff came in and out asking questions and checking their temperatures. After about an hour the man who'd been calling for Michael entered the room. Wrapped in heated blankets, the three boys were sipping hot chocolate and eating sandwiches. The man looked at them with tear-filled eyes.

"I don't know how I could ever possibly repay you for what you've done. I don't think you even comprehend what heroes you truly are. My son is going to be fine thanks to you. He's in the room next door sleeping," he said before pausing for a moment. "My name is Martin Whitman, and the boy you risked your lives to save is my only son, Michael. He's my entire world. We lost his mother two years ago and now all we have is each other." Martin's voice was choked.

The boys looked at him in surprise. They'd done what any other human being would do, hadn't they? But this man seemed to think they'd performed a great service.

"How long have you been living in the foster home over on Spruce?" Martin asked. Since Spence was the oldest—he was fourteen to Camden's thirteen and Jackson's twelve—he was the one to respond.

"We've been there for two years now."

Martin hesitated before he spoke again. "I talked with your social worker. She's on her way down here now. I'd like to make an offer to you boys."

They looked at him with distrustful eyes. They'd been in the foster-care system too long and had learned to trust no one but each other. They shared a common heartache—no one seemed to want any of them. Being alone was much better when you were "alone" with someone else. It had caused a unique bond to form—a brotherhood.

At least this man's eyes were kind. They waited in silence to see what he had to say.

"I'd like for you to come live with me. What you did today showed me more than I need to know about your characters, and I would be honored to adopt each of you. The judge here in town is a good friend of mine. He can give me temporary papers so you could come home with me right away. Then, if you like it at my place, we could make it permanent."

Spence took the lead again. "We've been lied to a lot. It would be pretty crappy of you to say something like this and then decide you hated us after a few days. They call us *throwaway kids* because we're older than kids who are typically adopted," he said with a slightly wobbly voice.

All of them were trying desperately to put up a brave front, but it was beginning to crumble as hope filled them. The pain that held all three of the boys in its grip was evident to Martin, whose heart filled with a deep sadness. What had they been through to be so wounded and so afraid? He hoped they never would have to carry that fear again.

"I understand that you don't know me, and it will take a lot of time to build up trust, but I don't lie and I never make a promise I don't keep. My father taught me to always be a man of my word. You three boys gave me the greatest gift today, one that only my wife had given me before now—the life of my son. Not everyone gets the kind of second chance you gave him. You deserve a second chance at life as well. I'd feel privileged to have you come home with me. You're not too old at all. My son is ten, right around your age. I think we could be a family if you give me a chance."

Spence immediately turned away when a tear started to slip down his cheek. The others pretended not to see and gave him a chance to pull himself together. They never cried, at least not where anyone else could see. They'd learned long ago that tears didn't matter from a throwaway kid anyway.

Martin Whitman did something then that no one had done for so long that the boys had forgotten what it felt like. He wrapped his arms around Spence and gave him a solid hug, and then did the same to Camden and to Jackson. All three boys were shaking with emotion by the time he let go.

Martin stood and walked to a nearby restroom so he could compose himself and give them a moment alone to discuss his offer.

"What do you think, Spence?" Jackson asked with a hopeful expression.

Spence looked at both Jackson and Camden, who stared back with a mixture of faith and disbelief. Though Jackson didn't want to get his hopes up, the thin layer of ice that encased his heart was beginning to thaw. He wanted to believe. He wanted this to be real. If Martin took them all, they would never be separated.

The rational part of him knew that a brighter tomorrow would never come. But for the sake of Camden and Spence, he put a confident smile on his face.

"I don't see what it would hurt to give it a try," he said.

Ultimately, the decision lay with Spence, though, since he was the oldest. They waited for his verdict.

"Why not?" he told them, trying to look composed, but excitement burned in his eyes.

Camden and Jackson beamed eager smiles his way, hopeful for the first time since they had been dumped at the state's doorstep when they were barely out of diapers.

When Martin emerged from the bathroom, Jackson and Camden looked at him with happy apprehension. Spence looked the man in the eye, issuing him a silent challenge: *this is me—take me or leave me.*

Martin smiled, not breaking eye contact for even a second, as if to reply that he would take him as he was, chip on his shoulder and all.

CHAPTER ONE

"I PROMISE YOU, MOM, I'm fine."

But Alyssa's mother kept on saying all the usual motherly things, full of worry and false cheer, not offering her daughter even the remotest chance of interrupting. Alyssa Gerard held her phone wearily against her ear. She had no more words to say, nothing that would make this nightmare end. A nine-hour flight was still ahead of her, then one connection, and she'd be home.

Or maybe not. Alyssa had waited in the crowded airport as her "on-time" flight was delayed again and again. It was already midafternoon, and she'd been in this boarding area for hours. Were there any other flights with open seats?

Not on this day of the year, New Year's Eve. She could either wait for her original flight, or give up—which wasn't going to happen. She was more than done with Paris, done with modeling, and done with people in general. This week had started out badly and kept on getting worse.

". . . and I know you'll really love it in Sterling . . ." Yes, her mom was still speaking, and yes, she should listen, but as she looked around at all the people in bright colors with what seemed like permanent smiles on their faces, she grew even grumpier and simply couldn't force herself to respond. Not that she needed to, as her mom was speaking enough for both of them. Alyssa should be happy, should feel like celebrating, but instead she was fighting tears.

". . . Martin is a wonderful boss. Your dad has never been happier . . ."

It was all over—everything had ended so much more speedily than it had begun. She'd set out at the tender age of fifteen, ready to change the world with all the millions she'd make, to see her name in lights, or at least to see her face on every magazine cover ever to grace store shelves and racks.

She'd gotten her dream . . . for a while. And then—poof!—it was gone. Her body tensed in anger as she found herself wedged between two large men who surely hadn't bathed in eons.

Her mother continued to yammer away, though Alyssa was long past listening.

". . . and you should see Martin's boys. They are so handsome . . ."

Shaking her head, she took a deep breath. To her left, a heated debate had broken out between a man in a dark blue suit and an attractive blonde. The exchange flung her back into her own head as she was forced to think about what had happened between her and her ex.

Her "trustworthy" manager, who'd also happened to be her boyfriend, had taken it all—he'd run away not only with her fortune but with her hopes and dreams and reputation. Now she was stuck in Paris on New Year's Eve, and all she could think about was how badly she wanted to be home, where she could lick her wounds in peace.

". . . your father and I are so excited to have you home. I only wish you'd been here last week. It was our first Christmas with snow . . ."

To top everything off with a nice, fat cherry, her parents had decided to move out of the thriving Texas town she'd grown up in and hare off to the backwoods of Montana, settling in a place she had never heard of before—Sterling. Her mother swore up and down they'd visited an aunt there several times when she was a kid, but the place must be awful because she couldn't even remember it.

Great! Just great. She had to go home with her tail tucked between her legs, and it wasn't even home. They had snow in Montana? Lots of snow? Like the sort of snow that buried people alive, and they weren't found again until months later, when the spring came and the roads finally cleared? She had a feeling she was going to be one of those unsuspecting victims—huddled in the fetal position as she froze to death in her car.

That is, if she was lucky enough to find a car she could afford.

". . . I've had quite a time learning to drive in snow, but it can actually be fun . . ."

Alyssa had heard some of this before. She still wasn't interested in living in Montana, not that she had a choice. She'd never thought she'd want that twenty-year-old Toyota so badly, but she was praying now that it had made the journey with her parents when they'd trekked north for her father's new job. Alyssa didn't even have enough money left to buy a five-hundred-dollar "preowned" lemon to get her to and from whatever job she'd manage to find back in the States.

". . . your dad sold the car, but I'm sure we can find you something when you get here . . ." Great. She didn't have the Toyota.

She could try to start again, try to make a go of a modeling career from scratch, but the reality was that she hated the industry, had hated it almost from the beginning, and now, at twenty-four, she was considered old in this world of the rich and beautiful, the sleek and connected. Connections that her manager/boyfriend had managed to sever irreparably.

"Honey? Are you still there?"

Alyssa jumped. She'd been sunk inside her own head so heavily that she'd forgotten her mom was on the phone.

"Mom, I love you and I promise I'm doing fine. I really appreciate the ticket home. But they're speaking to the passengers, so I have to hang up now."

With a little grumbling, her mother finally allowed her to disconnect her cell, though by then Alyssa had missed the agent's message. Scanning the seating by the gate, she promptly spotted a nice, quiet corner, one with no loud *or* sweaty men nearby, and made a beeline for it.

A few minutes later she heard a commotion and she glanced up to see an unhappy passenger arguing with one of the customer service agents. This wasn't anything new. Alyssa wasn't thrilled with the delay, either, but she'd been traveling a lot over the years and knew it was par for the course.

Would the passengers rather fly in an unsafe plane? Alyssa would prefer to fly with her mind at ease, and to land the same way. Delays were never fun, but she wasn't going to argue with people who knew a lot more about the airplanes than she did.

When several other people surged around the guy who'd gone ballistic—his voice was rising by the minute—and gained the "courage" to yell at the agent along with him, Alyssa tried not to watch. But it was like passing a wreck on the freeway. You knew it was ridiculous to slow down, but no matter how much you lectured yourself not to twist your head, it just seemed to happen.

As Alyssa focused on the clamor, she felt the air stir next to her as someone sat down. No rank odor assailed her, so she didn't pay attention to her new neighbor; she was busy watching two policemen walk to the customer service counter. The noise finally began dying down when the officers told the passengers that the next person to cause a problem would be escorted off the premises.

Nothing more to see there. She turned her head idly and then started in surprise; her eyes surely widened to the size of small saucers. Sitting next to her was a heart-stoppingly beautiful man—and she never used that term lightly. His thick, dark hair was cut just a little longer than was conventional, brushing the top of his ears. His solid jawline and high cheekbones gave him an air of natural sophistication, and the straight, smooth shape of his nose perfected his features.

But what really caught her attention were the sultry dark brown eyes with their perfect almond shape, and thick, long lashes that most people in her former industry would pay thousands of dollars to acquire. The man was positively delicious, which sent an instant shot of awareness through her stomach. And she had no business gazing his way.

Something was making him unhappy. His flawless lips were clamped in a straight line and his eyebrows bent inward in a scowl. When Alyssa finally exhaled, she found herself sitting up a little bit straighter. His scent was now dancing inside her, and—mmmm—whatever cologne the man was wearing was meant to seduce. Meant to make women turn their heads. And it was doing the trick on her.

"Mr. Whitman, is there anything else I can do for you?"

Alyssa turned to find one of the airline's agents hovering around her compelling neighbor. The name was familiar, but she couldn't place it.

"No. Leave me."

Wow! He *was* an unhappy man.

Alyssa decided that staying silent would be the wisest course of action. But she had never really been the silent type, and for some odd reason, this stranger's disgruntled mood made her feel less sorry for herself. It looked as if his day was going worse than hers. And *that* was saying a lot.

"I'm so sorry about the delay, Mr. Whitman," the agent said. "We'll be boarding within the next twenty minutes." When he didn't respond, she shifted on her feet before shuffling away.

The man's cold dismissal would make anyone uneasy. The little show that had just taken place told Alyssa that she should stand up quietly and find another seat. But she wouldn't. Not when she was suddenly so entertained right where she was.

The man was retrieving his laptop from his computer bag when the device slipped and he jerked his hand out to catch it; in the process, his elbow leapt over the armrest separating him from her and jabbed her in the ribs. She couldn't help giving out an *oof* of pain.

CHAPTER TWO

*C*OLD.
Untouchable.
Forbidding.

Those words described Jackson Whitman perfectly. It was the way he wanted to be viewed. It was safe—it protected him. After the loss of his daughter, he was done. Done with love. Done with playing nice. Done with it all.

People skirted around him, steered clear. Most people, that is. Certainly not his meddling family, who couldn't get it through their heads that he was now a lone wolf and preferred it that way. Of course, if they ever *actually* gave up on him, would he like that? He wanted to think that he would, but he knew the truth, knew he needed them. No one, however, would ever hear him say those words aloud.

Okay, he didn't need *companionship*; he didn't need long talks or people to be in his face. Sex, on the other hand—oh, yes, that need bubbled up inside him like molten lava boiling for an eternity in the confines of the earth, begging for release.

Right now, sex should be the last thing on his mind, but his neighbor, the woman he'd just managed to elbow, was making him unable to think of anything else. As he took in her pale blue eyes, sleek yet curvy body, silky reddish-blond hair, and ripe parted lips, sex was his only thought. Thrusting that thought away, he opened his mouth to apologize when her lips turned from an O to a smile.

"Well, that's certainly a new greeting," she said with a chuckle.

What the hell was she talking about? "Excuse me?"

"An apology would be expected, but you don't seem to be the sort of man who goes around apologizing, if your interaction with the airline employee is any indication of how you normally speak to strangers."

She wasn't being rude, exactly. She was just being . . . he couldn't quite put his finger on what the hell she was being. Jackson was used to women batting their eyelashes, licking their lips, leaning in to give him a clear invitation with a close-up of their cleavage. He wasn't used to anyone mocking him. It took him several silent seconds to form two words.

"I apologize."

"Wow. You really need to work on that."

Again he was floored. It was just as she'd said: he practically never apologized for anything. And she'd just thrown his sincere—all right, maybe not completely sincere, but still . . . She'd just thrown the words back at him without even a nod of her head indicating acceptance.

"It wasn't as if I intentionally elbowed you," he pointed out.

"I would hope not, since we don't know each other, and I've never done anything to warrant being hit by you," she said, the same grin in place.

"No woman should ever be hit." He wasn't amused.

"Ah, so you're a gentleman."

"I wouldn't go that far." And miraculously, he felt his lips turning up just the slightest bit. Sheesh, he couldn't remember the last time he'd smiled. Too much had happened in the past five years to make him feel like grinning.

"That's good to know, Mr. Whitman."

How did she know his name? Suspicion entered Jackson's thoughts. Then he remembered the rep who'd been busy kissing his ass. Airlines annoyed him. He hated flying commercial, preferring to use his jet, but one of his brothers was using it this week, and he'd had little choice but to come to Paris any way he could. He'd have put the trip off, but with the holidays, he'd been under certain pressing deadlines.

Now, inevitably, the flight was delayed, and here he was, sitting next to a distressingly intriguing woman. Dammit. Jackson didn't want to be intrigued, but it seemed as if his body had taken the reins from his brain.

That she'd mocked him gave him a measure of respect for her. It was refreshing to have a conversation with a woman who knew nothing about him, seemed to want nothing from him. He was tempted to change her mind on that front.

He loved sex.

Sex was healthy. It was vital. It's what kept this pathetic population going like the Energizer Bunny. Maybe this delay wouldn't end up being such an awful thing after all. But Jackson didn't jump into bed with women on a whim. Not usually, at least. He'd have to see how the next few minutes played out and then decide whether or not to bed her.

Yes, he was confident enough in himself to know that if he wanted her to share a bed with him, then she would indeed do so. He opened his laptop and pulled up a report. If she didn't speak again, maybe that would be the end of it. If she did . . . well, if she did, maybe he'd decide to prolong their conversation.

As he began working, a few minutes passed in total silence. So maybe their conversation was over; maybe that small stirring she'd caused in him had been nothing more than a fluke. But her scent began drifting over him. Fingers of jasmine and nutmeg twirled around his nose and slid across his cheeks. Taking a deep breath, he decided that work could wait for a while. There wasn't a lot of time before he and this nameless woman would board the plane.

As if his thoughts had caused the agents to actually do some work, an announcement came over the intercom, first in French, then in English. "Passengers outbound on Flight 28 with service to JFK, we apologize for the delay once again. We've been informed that boarding will begin in ten minutes. Please make your way back to gate K26 and we'll get through the boarding process quickly and have you on your way to New York in a timely fashion."

"Finally," she murmured, though she didn't seem particularly excited—most of the people in the terminal were clapping. She seemed to be practicing some sort of breathing exercises as she gripped her armrests. Was she afraid of flying?

"Thousands of flights take off and land safely every single day," Jackson said, almost surprised by the sound of his voice as he attempted to comfort her. Why would he care if she was frightened? It didn't affect him.

She turned her head slowly his way and her eyes were wide. "Yes, I know."

He waited, but she said nothing further. "Then why the panicked expression?"

"Probably because even though I know that flying is much safer than a car or boat, my brain won't listen to reason. Being thirty-something thousand feet in the air in a big metal machine is just unnatural," she replied before taking another long breath.

"I wouldn't say that boats are unsafe." Why had that popped from his mouth?

"Have you not watched *Titanic*? Or *Poseidon*? I'd say the passengers on those boats weren't too thrilled about how their ocean cruises ended," she said.

"The *Titanic* disaster could have been prevented, and *Poseidon* is fiction."

"Well, a lot of plane crashes could probably have been prevented, too, but with my luck I'm going to be on a flight that goes down in a fiery blaze of glory. Or simply disappears from radar, never to be seen again."

For some reason, she amused him. One minute she was all mocking and happy-go-lucky, and the next she seemed like a frightened teenager. Whatever she was, she wasn't boring.

"Why did you come all the way to Paris if you hate flying?"

"For work."

Her breathing had started to grow easier as they continued chatting, and that brought Jackson surprising pleasure. He liked that he was calming her, that the conversation they were having was taking her mind off her fears. Jackson performed billion-dollar deals on a regular basis. Deals of serious import and excitement. Calming a frightened woman wasn't in his job description and shouldn't matter to him in the least. But the fact was that it did matter.

"What kind of work?" he asked.

She tensed again.

"Nothing important," she said, then added, "I'm Alyssa, by the way. Alyssa Gerard."

She held out her hand and he looked at it as if it were a snake. With a strange reluctance, he held out his hand and clasped her fingers. He should have known better. As their fingers brushed together, a vibration of awareness rocketed right through him. That was all it had taken, one simple touch. This woman was dangerous.

Good thing he liked danger.

Just then his phone rang and he lifted it, his eyes not letting hers go. After a moment of listening, he gave a curt "No comment" and hung up. Damn reporters!

"Excuse me."

Without looking back at her, he stood and moved purposefully through the throng of eager passengers. Jackson always purchased two seats when he was forced to fly commercially. The last thing he wanted was to end up sitting on an eight- to twelve-hour flight next to some annoying stranger. In this case, his extra seat was an advantage.

"I want Alyssa Gerard moved to the open seat next to mine," Jackson said, handing over his boarding passes.

He always booked himself into the last row of first class, giving himself even more privacy. This trip, which hadn't begun well, was shaping up to be a lot more pleasant now that he had a sexy companion to pass the time with.

A predatory smile transformed his features, making the agent helping him blush. Now *that* was the reaction Jackson was used to receiving from women.

CHAPTER THREE

WHEN ALYSSA WAS called to the counter as preboarding was announced, she wondered what possibly could be going wrong now. Maybe her seat assignment had been lost or given away and she would be stuck in Paris forever.

Instead of being anxious, though, she turned her thoughts back to the stranger who'd bolted. But, today of all days, why was she thinking twice about the man? Maybe all the trauma had made her lose her mind, and it would be a mental ward she landed in instead of New York.

Having men lust after her was something Alyssa was used to. Most guys wanted to sleep with her, that was for sure. But it wasn't because they were in love with her. They either wanted to use her because they liked what they saw—not her, just her looks—or figured that it was a fashion model's duty to warm their beds.

It was almost inevitable in the world she'd been a part of. Modeling certainly hadn't brought her the life she'd expected. Her young dreams of fame, fortune, and glamour had earned her sackcloth and ashes, and she hadn't done anything wrong.

When she'd refused man after man, whether a coworker or a boss, she'd struggled in her career. Why should they deal with her when their working world abounded with exotic beauties who would do anything to further their careers?

It had taken her much longer to get the big break she'd been looking for, and then the ride hadn't lasted long. The one person she'd trusted . . .

A shudder ran through her. She refused to think about Carl Avone, her ex-boyfriend and manager. He was scum and wasn't worth the precious brain cells it would use to think of him again.

"Ms. Gerard, you've been upgraded to first class. Here's your new ticket."

Alyssa stood there in disbelief and stared at the agent, not moving to take the ticket. "Are you sure you have the right person?" she finally asked.

"Yes, ma'am." The woman didn't blink as she pushed the ticket closer.

"Seriously, I've had a hell of a week, and if I get on the plane in this seat and then they boot me out, I'm probably going to end up causing a riot," she warned the woman. She was impressed when the agent kept her smile in place.

"I assure you, Ms. Gerard, that the upgrade is legitimate."

Still suspicious, but not willing to appear ungrateful, Alyssa grabbed it and looked at the seat number with the words *de première classe*— "first class"—written in bold letters across the bottom.

Since she was left with virtually nothing, her parents had bought her a ticket to get home. There was no way they could afford a last-minute international first-class ticket. Feelings of guilt assailed Alyssa as she stepped away from the counter.

What if she was stealing someone's seat? Her name was printed on the pass, but how could she have been upgraded? She didn't even have a frequent-flier number. Her manager had always booked all her flights. Once in a blue moon she'd been placed in business class, which was heaven itself. But she'd never, *ever* flown first-class. It was a luxury she'd always wanted to enjoy.

First-class passengers were offered preboarding, and with only a small amount of hesitation she joined the line, feeling frumpy in her worn fitted jeans, wrinkled blouse, and baggy sweater. She'd been in a hurry to leave her small apartment and catch her flight home, and she had dressed quickly, packing the rest of her clothes for the journey.

Since she'd shared a place with several other models, it had been depressingly easy to move out; she owned only what she carried in her suitcases. Being a model, she had worn a lot of borrowed clothes to promote companies, and she played down her everyday appearance—she hadn't wanted to be recognized when not on the job.

better and better. Jackson seemed engrossed in his papers—he picked food off his plate without paying attention to what he was eating—but Alyssa didn't need him to entertain her.

He might be used to this life, and people might think a model was used to it, too, but only the lucky ones got this sort of treatment. She hadn't been in that mix. So she was going to enjoy every second and dream about it later.

If only her eyes would quit straying to the sensual man beside her, she'd have been a lot more pleased. But, hey, when a man looked that good, it was a law that he had to be looked at, right? Man candy, her mother would call him.

That thought made her giggle aloud, causing the man she was thinking about to turn his head, and suddenly she was caught by those simmering brown eyes.

Her Unexpected Hero is now available at all major retailers

CPSIA information can be obtained at www.ICGtesting.com
Printed in the USA
LVOW08s1927310516

490616LV00004B/207/P

None of the furniture had belonged to her, and she'd hung nothing on the walls. Sadly, she hadn't had so much as a single trinket in the apartment. The more she thought of her life as a model, the more she was grateful it was over. It just would have been nice if her exit from the business had been her choice. She would have come to the same place eventually, but she should have had a nice nest egg to fall back on.

As she entered the first-class cabin and spotted her seat, a smile of anticipation crossed her lips. Oh, this was definitely the way to fly! There was so much *room*. Plenty of space for her carry-on bag, her feet, her entire body. She might actually be able to catch a few hours of sleep. Not that she wanted to miss out on a moment of this experience, but she was exhausted from the sleepless nights this week, and then those frustrating hours of waiting in the terminal.

A blanket, pillow, and headphones were sitting in the large seat, and a bottle of water waited for her on the adjoining table. Putting her bag under the seat in front of her, she sat down with a wide smile as the flight attendant approached.

"Would you care for a drink?"

It had been hours since she'd ingested a single thing, and Alyssa desperately wanted something to eat and drink, but she didn't want to be a fool and ask whether there was a charge. All she had was the small emergency cash fund that she'd stuffed into her purse that morning, and she was holding on to *that* as tightly as humanly possible.

"Not right now," she replied. She'd have to look through the airline magazine first, find out whether precious dollars would be required.

"Let me know if you need anything before takeoff." With that, the pleasant flight attendant turned around and assisted other first-class passengers who were gradually filling up the cabin.

After grabbing the magazine, Alyssa was thrilled when she found the page describing first class. Not only were the drinks free, but so were the two meals she'd receive. Meals! Not just pretzels! Her stomach rumbled when she read the options.

"Mmm, this will be a nice flight," she murmured, feeling giddy and finding that she was having to stifle an excited giggle.

"I certainly hope so. It's been delayed long enough."

Alyssa's head snapped up to encounter a side view of Mr. Whitman as he slid into the aisle seat next to her.

"You're sitting here?" she asked, dumbfounded.

"I hope so," he said with a smirk as he placed his bag underneath the seat in front of his.

"Would you care for a drink?" The flight attendant was back, her smile just a bit more radiant than when she'd spoken to Alyssa a moment earlier.

"Yes, please. A gin and tonic," he answered, barely glancing at the woman.

"I've changed my mind," Alyssa said before the attendant could turn away. "I'll have a vodka and orange juice."

"I see you're in a much happier mood," her neighbor said.

Why was she sitting here? And why was he speaking to her? The last she'd seen of him had been the back of his head as he'd practically run away from her. So, of course, being a woman who didn't seem to have a filter when it came to speaking her mind, Alyssa had to make a comment.

"Do you always have that smirk on your face?"

He seemed startled by her question, but then he chuckled.

"I guess I do," he said before pausing for a few moments while he just looked at her with those intense eyes. "I never did introduce myself," he finally said, not holding his hand out this time. "Jackson Whitman."

The flight attendant returned with their drinks and Alyssa took a grateful sip. She definitely had to make the most of this. She'd never be able to afford first class again, and she hoped to heaven that it wouldn't kill her when she had to go back to the pits of coach.

Jackson pulled out some papers and read quietly while he sipped his beverage. Alyssa found her eyes glued to the small window next to her, the activity going on outside the plane oddly fascinating.

Bags were loaded, small carts darted around the tarmac, then the jet bridge was pulled back, and soon the airplane was gliding easily away from the gate. After the plane began moving forward, it wasn't long before they were racing down the runway and then lifting into the air.

This part had always made her clutch her seat in fear in the past, but now it was different. Maybe it was the smooth ascent. Maybe it was the comfort of her seat, or maybe the vodka had helped ease her fears. Whatever it was, her heart pounded only a little harder, and the hairs on the back of her neck weren't standing straight up.

Yep. This was going to be a great flight. Okay, it *would* be as long as she didn't think about the fact that they were high in the sky over a huge body of water that would prove harder than cement if they plummeted into it.

Nope. Alyssa wasn't going to think that way. The one and only time she flew first-class was not going to end with her becoming fish bait.

When the flight attendant brought an appealing plate of appetizers and placed it on her tray, Alyssa decided the night was just going to get